TANGLED THREAT

New York Times Bestselling Author

HEATHER GRAHAM

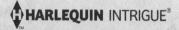

♦HARLEQUIN INTRIGUE®

For Roberta Young Peacock, a true Florida girl, with lots of
love and best wishes.

ISBN-13: 978-1-335-64105-2

Recycling programs
for this product may
not exist in your area.

Tangled Threat

Copyright © 2019 by Heather Graham Pozzessere

Printed in U.S.A.

www.Harlequin.com

He took a slight step back—almost as if he needed space.

"Brock, I never received any of your messages. I don't know if my parents thought they were protecting me... They're good people, but... I am so sorry. I really had it in for you for years—I thought you'd just walked away."

He shook his head. Shrugged. "Well, which room are you in?"

"I'm the last down the hallway. Number five," she said.

"I'll watch you through your door," he said with a half smile. "I mean, I'm here—might as well make sure you're perfectly safe."

"I assume I'll see you," she murmured.

"You will," he assured her.

She turned and headed down the small hallway to the end. There, she dug out her key, opened her door, waved and went in.

And finally, alone and in the sanctity of her room, she leaned against the door, shaking.

How could time erase their past so easily? How could the truth hurt so badly...and mean so very much at the same time? What would have happened if she had received his messages? Would they have been together all these years, perhaps with a little one now, or two little ones?

Just now, she could have turned to him, slipped her arms around him. She knew what it would feel like, knew how he'd hold her, cup her nape when he kissed her, knew the feel of his lips...

New York Times and *USA TODAY* bestselling author
Heather Graham has written more than a hundred
novels. She's a winner of the Romance Writers of
America's Lifetime Achievement Award, a Thriller
Writers' Silver Bullet and, in 2016, the Thriller Master
Award from ITS. She is an active member of
International Thriller Writers and Mystery Writers of
America, and is the founder of The Slush Pile Players,
an author band and theatrical group. An avid scuba
diver, ballroom dancer and mother of five, she still
enjoys her South Florida home, but also loves to travel.

For more information, check out her website,
theoriginalheathergraham.com, or find Heather on
Facebook.

Books by Heather Graham

Harlequin Intrigue

Undercover Connection
Out of the Darkness
Shadows in the Night
Law and Disorder
Tangled Threat

MIRA Books

The Seekers
The Summoning
A Lethal Legacy

And look for
The Stalking
coming soon!

Visit the Author Profile page at Harlequin.com.

CAST OF CHARACTERS

Maura Antrim—The video producer is back at Frampton Ranch and Resort for the first time since she was a teenager working there for the summer and discovered the body of a coworker hanging in the woods.

Brock McGovern—A wrongful accusal twelve years ago set this FBI agent on a path that didn't include his girlfriend, Maura.

Angie Parsons—An author who works with Maura to create web content, she's obsessed with the strange and violent histories of some Florida landmarks.

Donald Glass—The smooth and sophisticated resort developer is well liked by his staff. Maybe too well liked, in someone's opinion.

Marie Glass—Donald's wife is a steadfast fixture at the Florida property.

Nils and Mark Hartford—The brothers were once snobby teens at the resort but now work there as the restaurant manager and a tour guide.

Fred Bentley—The resort manager has been there forever. Does he know, quite literally, where the skeletons are buried?

Detective Rachel Lawrence—The rookie investigator also has ties to the resort, though she's changed a lot in the passing years.

Detective Michael Flannery—As a junior detective back in the day, he was quick to arrest Brock. Now he's determined to solve the murders once and for all.

Prologue

The History Tree

"They see her…the beautiful Gyselle, when the moon is high in the sky. She walks these oak-lined trails and sometimes pauses to touch the soft moss that drips from the great branches, as if she reaches out for them to touch what is real. In life she was kind and generous. She was beloved by so many. And yet, when brought so cruelly to her brutal and unjust death at the infamous History Tree, she cast a curse on those around her. Those involved would die bitter deaths as well, choking on their own blood, breath stolen from them as it had been from her," Maura Antrim said dramatically.

The campfire in the pit burned bright yellow and gold, snapping and crackling softly. All around them, great oaks and pines rose, moss

swaying in the light breeze. The moon over-
head was full and bright that night, but cloud
cover drifted past now and then, creating eerie
shadows everywhere.

It was a perfect summer night, and perfect
for storytelling. She was glad to be there, glad
to be the storyteller and glad of the response
from her audience.

Maura's group from the resort—teenagers
and adults alike—looked at her, wide-eyed.

She refused to smile—she wanted to remain
grave—though she was delighted by the fascination of the guests assembled around her.
She had been grateful and pleased to be upgraded to her position of storyteller for the
Frampton Ranch and Resort, an enterprise in
North Central Florida that was becoming more
renowned daily as a destination. The property
had been bought about five years back by bil-
lionaire hotelier Donald Glass, and he had
wisely left the firepit and the old riding trails
as they were, the History Tree right where it
grew, the ruins of the old plantation just as
they lay—and amped up the history first, and
then the legends that went along with the area.

Maura wasn't supposed to be on tonight—
she shared the position with Francine Renault,

a longtime employee of Donald Glass's hotel corporation, probably second in command only to the main resort manager, Fred Bentley. The two of them were known to argue—but Francine stayed right where she was, doing what she wanted. Despite any arguments, Donald Glass refused to fire either Francine or Fred, who, despite his stocky bulk, moved around the resort like a bat out of hell, always getting things done.

Fred Bentley had watched Maura at the start of the evening; she thought that he was smiling benignly—that he approved of her abilities as a social hostess and storyteller.

It was hard to blame him for fighting with Francine. She was…a difficult personality type at best.

And sharing any job with Francine wasn't easy; the woman had an air of superiority about her and a way of treating those she considered to be "lesser" employees very badly. Francine was in her midthirties—and was a beauty, really, a platinum blonde, dark-eyed piece of perfection—and while Maura had turned eighteen, Francine considered all of Donald Glass's summer help annoying, ignorant children.

The young adults—or "camper" summer help—were fond of gossiping. It was rumored that Francine once had an affair with Donald Glass, and that was how she held on to her position—and her superiority.

Glass was married. Maybe Francine was blackmailing him, telling him that if she wasn't given a certain power, she'd tell his wife, Marie, and Marie—or so rumor had it—could be jealous and very threatening when she chose to be. Hard to believe—in public Marie was always the model of decorum, slim and regal, slightly younger than Donald but certainly older than Francine.

Teens and young adults loved to speculate. At Maura's age, the thought of any of the older staff together—all seeming so much older than she was at the time—was simply gross.

Tonight, by not being there, Francine had put herself in a bad position.

She hadn't shown up for work. A no-show without a call was grounds for dismissal, though Maura seriously doubted that Francine would be fired.

Maura looked around, gravely and silently surveying her group before beginning again.

She didn't get a chance—someone spoke up. A young teenager.

"They should call it the Torture Tree or the Hangman's Tree…or something besides the History Tree," he said.

The boy's name was Mark Hartford, Maura thought. She'd supervised a game at the pool one day when he had been playing. He was a nice kid, curious and, maybe because he was an adolescent boy, boisterous. He also had an older brother, Nils—in college already. Mark's brother wasn't quite as nice; he knew that many of the workers were his own age or younger, and he liked to lord his status as a guest over them. He was bearable, however.

"The Torture Tree! Oh, lord, you little…heathen!"

Nils had a girlfriend. Rachel Lawrence. She was nicer than Nils, unless Nils was around. Then she behaved with a great deal of superiority, as well. But, Maura realized, Nils and Rachel *were* at the campfire that night—they had just joined quietly.

Quietly—which was amazing in itself. Nils liked to make an entrance most of the time, making sure that everyone saw him.

Rachel had her hands set upon Mark's

shoulders—even as she called him a heathen. She looked scared, or nervous maybe, Maura thought. Maybe it was for effect; Nils set his arm around her shoulders, as a good, protective boyfriend should. They made a cute family picture, a young adult male with his chosen mate and a young one under their wings.

Maura was surprised they were on the tour. Nils had said something the other day about the fact that they were too mature for campfire ghost stories.

"Torture Tree—yes, that would be better!" Mark said. He wasn't arguing with Rachel, he was determined that he was right. "Poor Gyselle—she was really tortured there, right?"

Mark and the other young teens were wide-eyed. Teenagers that age liked the sensational—and they liked it grisly.

"She was dragged there and hanged, so yes, I'm sure it was torture," Maura said. "But it was the History Tree long before a plantation was built here, years and years ago," Maura said. "That was the Native American name for it—the Timucua were here years before the Spanish came. They called it the History Tree, because even back then, the old oak had grown together with a palm, and it's been that way since. Anyway, we'll be seeing the History Tree soon enough," she said softly. "The tree that first welcomed terror when the beautiful Gyselle was tormented and hanged from the tree until dead. And where, so they say, the hauntings and horrors of the History Tree began."

Maura saw more than one of her audience members glance back over the area of sweeping, manicured lawn and toward the ranch, as if assuring themselves that more than the night and the spooky, draped trees existed, that there was light and safety not far away.

The new buildings Donald Glass had erected were elegant and beautiful. With St. Augustine just an hour and a half in one direction and Disney and Universal and other theme parks just an hour and half to the south—not to mention a nice proximity to the beaches and racetrack at Daytona and the wonder of Cape Kennedy being an hour or so away, as well—Frampton Ranch and Resort was becoming a must-see location.

Still, the ranch had become renowned for offering Campfire Ghost Histories. Not stories, but histories—everything said was history and fact…to a point.

The listeners could hear what people claimed to have happened, and they could believe—or not. And then they'd walk the trails where history had occurred.

"You see, Gyselle had been a lovely lost waif, raised by the Seminole tribe after they found her wandering near the battlefield at the end of the Second Seminole War. She was 'rescued' by Spanish missionaries at the beginning of the Third Seminole War, though, at that point, she probably didn't want or need rescuing, having been with a Seminole family for years. But 'saved' and then set adrift, she found work at the old Frampton plantation, and there she caught the eye of the heir, and despite his arranged marriage to socialite Julie LeBlanc, the young Richard Frampton fell head over heels in love with Gyselle. They were known to escape into the woods where they both professed their love, despite all the odds against them—and Richard's wife, Julie. Knowing of her husband's infidelity, Julie LeBlanc arranged to poison her father-in-law—and let the blame fall on Gyselle. Gyselle was hunted down as a murderous witch, supposedly practicing a shaman's magic or a form of voodoo—it was easy to blame it on traditions the plantation workers didn't really understand—and she was hanged there, from what was once a lover's tree where she had met with Richard, her love, who had promised to protect her..."

She let her voice trail. Then she finished.

"Here, in these woods, Gyselle loved, not wisely, but deeply. And here she died. And so they say, when the moon has risen high and full in the night sky—as it is now—those who walk the trails by night can hear her singing softly 'The Last Rose of Summer' with a lovely Irish lilt to her voice."

"What about the curse?" a boy cried out.

"Yeah, the curse! That she spoke before she died—swearing that her tormenters would choke on their own blood! You just said that she cursed everyone, and there are more stories, right?" Mark—never one to be silent long—asked eagerly.

Maura felt—rather than saw—Brock McGovern at her side. He was amused. Barely eighteen, he'd nevertheless been given the position of stage manager for events such as the campfire history tour. He'd been standing to one side just behind her as she told her tale with just the right dramatic emphasis—or so she believed.

He stepped forward, just a shade closer, nearly touching her.

"Choking on their own blood? Kind of a standard curse, huh?" he teased softly and for her ears alone.

Maura ignored him, trying not to smile, and still, even here, now, felt the rush she always did when Brock was around.

Brock was always ready to tease—but also to encourage and support whatever she was doing. He had that ability and the amazing tendency to exude an easy confidence that stretched far beyond his years. But he was that sure of himself. He was about to leave for the service, and when he returned, he planned to go to college to study criminology. Barely an adult, he knew what he wanted in life. She was sure he was going to work hard during basic training; he'd work hard through the college or university of his choice. And then he'd make up his mind just where he wanted to serve— FBI, US Marshals, perhaps even Homeland Security or the Secret Service.

He shook his head, smiling at her with his unusual eyes—a shade so dark that they didn't appear brown at times, but rather black. His shaggy hair—soon to become a buzz cut—was as dark as his eyes, and it framed a face that was, in Maura's mind, pure enchantment. He had already had a fine, steady chin—the kind most often seen on more mature men. His cheekbones were broad, and his skin was continually bronzed. He was, in her mind, beautiful.

He'd often told the tales himself, and he did so very well. He had a deep, rich voice that could rise and fall at just the right moments—a voice that, on its own, could awaken every sense in Maura's body. They had known each other for three years now, laughed and joked together, ridden old trails, worked together... always flirting, nearly touching at first, but always aware that, when summer ended, he would head back down to Key West and she would return to West Palm Beach—about 233 miles apart, just a little too far for a high school romance.

But this summer...

Things had changed.

She had liked him from the time she had met him; she had compared any other young man she met to him, and in her mind, all others fell short. He'd been given a management job that summer, probably because he was always willing to pitch in himself, whether it came to working in the restaurant when tables needed bussing or hauling in boxes when deliveries arrived. He'd gained a lean and muscular physique from hard work as much as from time in the gym, and he had a quick mind and a quicker wit, cared for people, was generous with his time, and was just...

Perfect. She'd never find anyone so perfect in life again, Maura was certain, even though she knew that her mother and father smiled indulgently when she talked about him in glowing terms—she was, after all, just eighteen, with college days and so much more ahead of her.

This summer they'd become a true couple. In every way.

A very passionate couple.

They'd had sex, in her mind, the most amazing sex ever, more meaningful than any sex had ever been before.

Just the thought brought a rush of blood to her face.

But...she believed that they would go on even through their separation, no matter the distance, no matter what. People would think, of course, that she was just a teenager, that she couldn't be as madly in love as she believed she was. So she was determined that no one would really realize just how insanely fully she did love him.

She turned to Brock. He was smiling at her. Something of a secret smile, charming, sexy… a smile that seemed to hint that they always shared something unique, something special.

She grinned in return.

Yep. He had become her world.

"Take it away," she told him.

"The curse!" he said, stepping in with a tremor in his voice. "It's true that while being dragged to the tree—which you'll see soon on our walk—the poor woman cried out that she was innocent of any cruel deed, innocent of murder. And she said that those who so viciously killed her would die in agony and despair. The very woods here would be haunted for eternity, and the evil they perpetrated on her would live forever. They had brought the devil into the woods, and there he would abide."

He smiled, innately charming when he spoke to a group, and continued, "I think that storytellers have added in the choking-on-blood part. Very dramatic and compelling, but... there are records of the occasion of the poor woman's demise available at the resort library." He set his flashlight beneath his chin, creating an eerie look.

"And," Maura said, "what is also documented is that bad things continued to happen on the ranch—under the same tree, the condemned killer, Marston Riggs, tortured and killed his victims in the early 1900s, and as late as 1970, the man known as the Red Tie Killer made use of the tree as well, killing five men and women at the History Tree and leaving their bones to fall to the ground. But, of course, we don't believe in curses. The History Tree and the ranch are perfectly safe nowadays..." She looked at Brock. "Shall we?" she asked.

"Indeed, we shall," he said, and the sound of his voice and the look that he gave her made her long for it to be later, when they had completed the nighttime forest tour—and were alone together.

They walked by the grove, where there was a charming little pond rumored to invigorate life—a handsomely written plaque commemorating the Spaniard Reynaldo Montenegro and his exploration of Florida.

Brock said to the tour group, "Here we are at the famous grove where Reynaldo Montenegro claimed to have found the Pond of Eternal Youth."

It was as great tour; even the adolescents continued to ask questions as they walked.

"I'm happy to have been the tour guide tonight," Maura murmured to Brock. "But I can't believe that Francine just didn't show up."

"If I know Francine, she'll make a grand entrance somewhere along the line, with a perfect reason for not being on time. She'll have some mammoth surprise for everyone—something way more important than speaking to the guests. Hey, what do you want to bet that we see her somewhere before this tour is over? Here, folks," Brock announced, "you'll see the plaque—an inquisition did come to the New World!"

The copse, illuminated only by the sparkling lights that lit the trail, offered a sadder message—that of tortures carried out by an invading society on the native population it encountered.

They passed the ruins of an old Spanish farm and then they neared the tree.

The infamous History Tree.

The tree—or trees—older than anyone could remember, stood dead center in the small clearing, as if nothing else would dare to grow near. Gnarled and twisted together, palm and oak suggested a mess of human limbs, coiled together in agony.

Maura stopped dead, hearing a long, terrified scream, then realizing that she'd made the sound herself.

From one large oaken branch, a body was hanging, swaying just slightly in the night breeze.

She didn't need to wonder why Francine Renault had been derelict in her duty.

She was there...part of the tour, just not as she should have been.

Head askew, neck broken. She was hanging there, in the place where others had been hanged through the years, again and again, where they had decayed, where their bones had dotted the earth beneath them.

Brock had been right.

Francine Renault had indeed shown up before the tour was over.

THE POLICE FLOODED the ranch with personnel, the medical examiner and crime scene technicians.

The rich forest of pines and oaks and ferns and earth became alive with artificial light, and still, where the moss sagged low, the bright beams just made the night and the macabre situation eerier.

Detective Michael Flannery had been put in charge of the case. Employees and guests had been separated and then separated again, and eventually, Maura sat at the edge of the parking lot, shivering although it wasn't cold, waiting for the officer who would speak with her.

When he got there, he wanted to know the last time she had seen Francine. She told him it had been the night before.

Where she had been all day? In the office, in the yard with the older teen boys and at the campfire.

Had she heard anyone threaten Francine?

At least half of the resort's employees. In aggravation or jest.

The night seemed to wear on forever.

When she was released at last, she was sent

back to her own room and ordered to stay there until morning.

When morning came, her parents were there, ready to take her home.

She desperately wanted to see Brock.

Her parents were quiet and then they looked at each other. Her father shook his head slightly, and her mother said softly, "Maura, you can't see Brock."

"What?" she demanded. "Why not? Mom, Dad—I'm about to leave home. Go to college, really be on my own. I love you. I'm going to come home. But… I'm almost eighteen. I won't go without seeing Brock."

Her father, a gentle giant with broad shoulders and a mane of white hair, spoke to her softly. "Sweetheart, we didn't say that we wouldn't let you see Brock. We're saying that you *can't* see Brock." He hesitated, looking over at her mother, and then he continued with, "I'm so sorry. Brock was arrested last night. He was charged with the murder of Francine Renault."

And with those words, it seemed that her world fell apart, that what she had known, that what she had believed in, all just exploded into a sea of red and then disappeared into smoke and fog.

what she had believed in, all rests, crushed in pieces of red, curling from displays, spilling smoke and fog.

Chapter One

"I'm assigned to go back to Florida. To stay at the Frampton Ranch and Resort—and investigate what we believe to be three kidnappings and a murder. And the kidnappings may have nothing to do with the resort, nor may the murder?" Brock McGovern asked, a small note of incredulity slipping into his voice, which was surprising to him—he was always careful to keep an even tone.

FBI Assistant Director Richard Egan had brought him into his office, and Brock had known he was going on assignment—he just hadn't expected this.

"Yes, not what you'd want, but, hey, maybe it'll be good for you—and perhaps necessary now, when time is of the essence and there is no one out there who could know the place or the circumstances with the same scope and experience you have," Egan told him. "Three young women have disappeared from the area. Two of them were guests of the Frampton Ranch and Resort shortly before their disappearances—the third had left St. Augustine and was on her way there. The Florida Department of Law Enforcement has naturally been there already. They asked for federal help on this. Shades of the past haunt them—they don't want any more unsolved murders—and everyone is hoping against hope that Lily Sylvester, Amy Bonham and Lydia Merkel might be found."

"These are Florida missing persons cases," Brock said. "And it's sad but true that young people go to Florida and get caught up in the beach life and the club scene. And regrettable but true once again—there's a drug and alcohol culture that does exist and people get caught up in it. Not just in Florida, of course, but…everywhere." He smiled grimly. "I go where I'm told, but I'm curious—how is this an FBI affair? And forgive me, but FBI out of New York?"

"Not out of New York. FDLE asked for you. Specifically."

"I see."

Egan didn't often dwell on the emotional or psychological, but the assistant director hesitated and then said, "You could put your past to rest."

Brock shrugged. "You know, one of the cooks committed suicide not long after the murder. Peter Moore. He stabbed himself with a butcher knife. He'd had a lot of fights with Francine Renault—the victim found at the tree. They suspected he might have killed himself out of remorse."

Egan offered him a dry grimace. "I know about the cook, of course. You know me—I knew everything about you on paper before I took you into this unit. I'm not sure anyone would have made a case against him in court. That's all beside the point—the past may well be the past. But there's the now, as well. They're afraid of a serial killer, Brock," Egan said. And he continued with, "The badly decomposed remains—mostly bones—of another young woman who went missing several months ago were recently found in a bizarre way—they were dumped in with sheets from several hotels and resorts at an industrial laundry that accepted linens from dozens of places—Frampton Ranch and Resort being one of them."

"I see," Brock said.

He didn't really see.

That didn't matter; Egan would be thorough.

"Yes, this may be a bit hard on you, but you're the one in the know. To come close to a knowledge of the area and people that you already have might take someone else hours or days that may cost a life… You're the best man for this. Especially because you were once falsely accused. And, I believe, you may just solve something of the mystery of the past. And quit hating your own home."

"I don't hate my own home. Ah, come on, sir, I don't want to play any cure-me psychological games with this," Brock said.

Egan shook his head and leaned forward, his eyes narrowed—indicating a rise in his temper, something always kept in check. "If I thought you needed to be cured, you wouldn't be in my unit. Women are missing. They might be dead already," he said curtly. "And then again, they might have a chance. You're the agent with a real sense for the place, the people and the surrounding landscape. And you're a good agent, period. I trust in your ability to get this sorted."

Brock greatly admired Egan. He had a nose for sending the right agent or agents in for a job. Usually.

But Brock was sitting across from Egan in Egan's office—in New York City. He, Brock, was an NYC agent.

And while Brock really didn't dislike where he came from—he still loved Florida, especially his family home in the Keys—he had opted to apply to the New York office of the Bureau specifically because it was far, far away from the state of his birth.

The New York City office didn't usually handle events in Florida, unless a criminal had traveled from New York down to the southern state. Florida had several field offices—including a multimillion-dollar state-of-the-art facility in Broward County. That was south—but Orlando had an exceptional office, close enough to the Frampton place. And there were more offices, as well.

Even if the Frampton Ranch and Resort was in a relatively isolated part of the state, a problem there would generally be handled by a more local office.

"Frampton Ranch and Resort," he heard himself say. And this time, years of training and experience kicked in—his voice was perfectly level and emotionless.

It was true: he sure as hell knew it and the area. The resort was just a bit off from—or maybe part of—what people considered to be the northern Ocala region, where prime acreage was still available at reasonable prices, where horse ranches were common upon the ever-so-slightly rolling hills and life tended to be slow and easy.

There were vast tracts of grazing ground and great live-oak forests and trails laden with pines where the sun seemed to drip down through great strands of weeping moss that hung from many a branch. It could be considered horse country, farm country and ranch county. There were marshes and forests, sinkholes and all manner of places where a body might just disappear.

The Frampton ranch was north of Ocala, east of Gainesville and about forty-five minutes south of Olustee, Florida, where every year, a battle reenactment took place, drawing tourists and historians from near and far. The Battle of Olustee, won by forces in the state;

the war had been heading toward its final inevitable conclusion, and then time proved that victory had been necessary for human rights and the strength and growth of the fledgling nation, however purposeless the sad loss of lives always seemed.

Reenactors and historians arrived in good numbers, and those who loved bringing history to life also loved bringing in crowds and many came for the campgrounds. The reenactment took place in February, when temperatures in the state tended to be beautiful and mosquito repellent wasn't as much a requirement as usual. During the winter season—often spring break for other regions—the area was exceptionally popular.

The area was beautiful.

And the large areas of isolation, which included the Frampton property, could conceal any number of dark deeds.

He'd just never thought he'd go back to it.

Certainly, time—and the path he had chosen to take in life—had helped erase the horror of the night they had come upon the body of Francine Renault hanging from the History Tree and his own subsequent arrest. He'd been so young then, so assured that truth spoke for

itself. In the end, his parents—bless them—
had leaped to the fore, flying into action, and
their attorney had made quick work of getting
him out of jail after only one night and seeing
that his record was returned to spotless. It was
ludicrous that they had arrested him; he'd been
able to prove that it would have been impossible for him to have carried out the deed. Dozens of witnesses had attested to the fact that he
couldn't have been the killer, he'd been seen
by so many people during the hours in which
the murder must have taken place. He could
remember, though, sitting in the cell—cold,
stark, barren—and wondering why in God's
name they had arrested *him*.

He discovered that there had been an anonymous call to the station—someone stating that
they had seen him dragging Francine Renault
into the woods. The tipster had sworn that he
would appear at a trial as a witness for the
prosecution, but the witness had not come to
the station. Others had signed formal protests,
and the McGoverns' attorney had taken over.

So many people had come forward, indignant, furious over his arrest.

But not Maura. She had been gone. Just
gone. He couldn't think of the Frampton Ranch

and Resort without a twinge of pain. He had never been sure which had broken him more at the time—the arrest or the fact that Maura had disappeared as cleanly from his life as any hint of daylight once night had fallen.

They had been so young. It had been natural that her parents whisked her away, and maybe even natural that neither had since tried to reach the other.

But there were times when he could still close his eyes and see her smile and be certain that he breathed in the subtle scent of her. Twelve years had gone by; he wasn't even the same person.

Egan was unaware of his reflections.

"Detective Michael Flannery is lead investigator now. He was on the case when you were arrested for the crime, but he wasn't lead."

"I know Flannery. We've communicated through the years, believe it or not. I almost feel bad—he suffered a lot of guilt about jumping the gun with me."

"He's with the Florida Department of Law Enforcement now, with some seniority and juice, so it seems," Egan informed him. "Years ago, when the murder took place, the federal government wasn't involved. Flannery doesn't want this crime going unsolved. He knows you're in this office now. His commander told me that he keeps in touch with you." Egan paused. "It doesn't sound as if you have a problem with him—you don't, right?"

"No, sir, I do not."

Even as a stunned kid—what he had been back then—Brock had never hated Detective Flannery for being one of the men who had come and arrested him.

Flannery had been just as quick to listen to the arguments that eventually cleared Brock completely of any wrongdoing. While Brock knew that Flannery was furious that he had been taken and certain that there had been an underlying and devious conspiracy to lead him and his superiors so thoroughly in the wrong direction, he had to agree that, at the time, Brock had appeared to be a ready suspect.

He'd had a fight with Francine that day, and it had been witnessed by many people. He hadn't gotten physical in any way, but his poor opinion of her, and his anger with her, had probably been more than evident—enough for him to be brought in for questioning and to be held for twenty-four hours at any rate.

"I'm curious how something that happened

so long ago can relate to the cases happening now," Brock said.

"It may not. The remains of the dead girl found in the laundry might have been the work of one crazed individual or an acquaintance seeking vengeance, acting out of jealousy—a solitary motive. It might be coincidence the way she was found—or maybe a killer was trying to throw suspicion upon a particular place or person. But…a lot of the same individuals are still there now who were there when Francine Renault was killed."

"Donald Glass—he's around a lot, though he does spend time at his other properties. Fred Bentley—I imagine he's still running the works. Who else is still there?" Brock asked.

Egan handed him a pile of folders. "All this is coming to your email, as well. There you have those who are in residence—and dossiers on the victims. Yes, Glass and Bentley are still on the property. There are other staff members who never left—Millie Cranston, head of Housekeeping. Vinnie Marshall, upgraded to chef—after Peter Moore's death, I might add. And then…" He paused, tapping the folders. "You have some old guests who are now employees."

"Who?"

"Mark and Nils Hartford," Egan told him. "Both of them report directly to Fred Bentley. Mark has taken over as the social director. Nils is managing the restaurants—the sit-down Ranch Roost and the Java Bar."

Brock hadn't known that the Hartford brothers—who'd seemed so above the working class when they'd been guests—were now employed at the very place where they had once loved to make hell for others.

"Flannery said this is something he hadn't mentioned to you. One of your old friends—or acquaintances—Rachel Lawrence is now with FDLE. She's been working the murder and the disappearances with him."

"Rachel? Became…a cop?" Brock shook his head, not sure if he was angry or amused. Rachel had never wanted to break a nail. She'd been pretty and delicate and… She'd also been a constant accessory of Nils Hartford.

"I guess your old friend Flannery was afraid to tell you."

"I don't know why he would be. I'm just a little surprised—she seemed more likely to be on one of those shows about rich housewives in a big city, but I never had a problem with her. That the Hartford brothers both became employees—that's also a surprise. They made me think of *Dirty Dancing*. They were the rich kids—we were the menial labor. But the world changes. People change."

"Flannery's point, so it appears, is that a number of the same players are in the area— may mean something and may not. There have been, give or take, approximately a thousand murders in the state per year in the last years. But that's only about four percent per the population. Still, anything could have happened. Violent crime may have to do with many factors—often family related, gang related, drug related, well…you know all the drills. But if we do have a serial situation down there—relating to or not relating to the past—everyone needs to move quickly. Not only do you know the area and the terrain, you know people and you know the ropes of getting around many of the people and places who might be integral to the situation."

"Yes. And any agent would want to put a halt to this—put an end to a serial killer. Or find the girls—alive, one can pray—or stop future abductions and killings."

Egan nodded grimly and tossed a small pile

of photos down before him. Brock could see three young, hopeful faces looking back at him. All three were attractive, and more grippingly, all three seemed to smile with life and all that lay before someone at that tender age.

"The missing," Egan said. He had big hands and long fingers. He used them to slide the first three photographs over.

The last was a divided sheet. On one side was the likeness of a beautiful young woman, probably in her early twenties. Her hair had been thick and dark and curly; her eyes had been sky blue. Her smile had been engaging.

"Maureen Rodriguez," Egan said. He added softly, "Then and now."

On the other side of the divided sheet was a crime scene photo—an image of bones, scattered in dirt in a pile of sheets. In the center of the broken and fragmented bones was a skull.

The skull retained bits of flesh.

"According to the investigation, she was on her way to Frampton Ranch and Resort," Egan said.

Brock nodded slowly and rose. "As am I," he said. "When do I leave?"

"Your plane is in two hours—down to Jacksonville. You've a rental car in your name when you arrive. I'm sure you know the way to the property. Detective Flannery will be waiting to hear from you. He'll go over all the particulars."

Brock was surprised to see that Egan was still studying him. "You are good, right?" he asked Brock.

"Hey, everyone wants to head to Florida for the winter, don't they?" he asked. "I'm good," he said seriously. "Maybe you're right. Maybe we can put the past to rest after all."

"I LOVE IT—just love it, love it, love it! Love it all!" Angie Parsons said enthusiastically. She offered Maura one of her biggest, happiest smiles.

She was staring at the History Tree, her smile brilliant and her enthusiasm for her project showing in the brightness of her eyes and her every movement. "I mean, people say Florida has no history—just because it's not New England and there were no pilgrims. But, hey, St. Augustine is—what?—the oldest settlement continually…settled…by Europeans in the country, right? I mean, way back, the Spaniards were here. No, no, the state wasn't one of the original thirteen colonies. No, no Puritans here. But! There's so much! And this tree... No one knows how old the frigging oak is or when the palm tree grew in it or through it or with it or whatever."

Angie Parsons was cute, friendly, bright and sometimes, but just sometimes, too much. At five feet two inches, she exuded enough energy for a giant. She had just turned thirty—and done brilliantly for her years. She had written one of the one most successful nonfiction book series on the market. And all because she got as excited as she did about objects and places and things—such as the History Tree.

The main tree was a black oak; no one knew quite how old it was, but several hundred years at least. That type of oak was known to live over five hundred years.

A palm tree had—at some time—managed to grow at the same place, through the outstretched roots of the oak and twirling up around the trunk and through the branches. It was bizarre, beautiful, and so unusual that it naturally inspired all manner of legends, some of those legends based on truth.

And, of course, the History Tree held just the kind of legend that made Angie as successful as she was.

Angie's being incredibly successful didn't hurt Maura any.

But being here... Yes, it hurt. At least... it was incredibly uncomfortable. On the one hand it was wonderful seeing people she had worked with once upon a time in another life.

On the other hand it was bizarre. Like visiting a mirror dimension made up of things she remembered. The Hartford brothers were working there now. Nils was managing the restaurants—he'd arrived at the table she and Angie had shared last night to welcome them and pick up their dinner check. Of course, Nils had become management. No lowly posts for him. He seemed to have an excellent working relationship with Fred Bentley, who was still the manager of the resort. Bentley had come down when they'd checked in—he'd greeted Maura with a serious hug. She was tall, granted, and in heels, and he was on the short side for a man—about five-ten—but it still seemed that his hug allowed for him to rest his head against her breasts a moment too long.

But still, he'd apparently been delighted to see her.

And Mark Hartford had come to see her, too, grown-up, cute and charming now—and just as happy as his brother to see her. It was thanks to her, he had told her, and her ability to tell the campfire histories, that had made him long to someday do the same.

The past didn't seem like any kind of a boulder around his neck. Certainly he remembered the night that Francine had been murdered.

The night that had turned *her* life upside down had been over twelve years ago.

Like all else in the past, it was now history.

Time had marched on, apparently, for them—and her.

She'd just turned eighteen the last time she had been here. When that autumn had come around, she'd done what she'd been meant to do, headed to the University of Central Florida, an amazing place to study performance of any kind and directing and film—with so many aspects thrown into the complete education.

She'd spent every waking minute in classes—taking elective upon elective to stay busy. She was now CEO of her own company, providing short videos to promote writers, artists, musicians and anyone wanting video content, including attorneys and accountants.

Not quite thirty, she could be proud of her

professional accomplishments—she had garnered a great reputation.

She enjoyed working with Angie. The writer was fun, and there was good reason for her success. She loved the bizarre and spooky that drew human curiosity. Even those who claimed they didn't believe in anything even remotely paranormal seemed to love Angie's books.

Most of the time, yes, Maura *did* truly enjoy working with Angie, and since Angie had tried doing her own videos without much success, she was equally happy to be working with Maura. They'd done great bits down in Key West at the cemetery there—where Maura's favorite tomb was engraved with the words *I told you I was sick!*—and at the East Martello Museum with Robert the Doll. They had filmed on the west coast at the old summer estates that had belonged to Henry Ford and Thomas Edison. And they'd worked together in St. Augustine, where they'd created twenty little video bits for social media that had pleased Angie to no end—and garnered hundreds of thousands of hits.

Last night, even Marie Glass—Donald's reserved and elegant wife—had come by their dinner table to welcome them and tell them just how much she enjoyed all the videos that Maura had done for and with Angie, telling great legends and wild tales that were bizarrely wonderful—and true.

Maybe naturally, since they were working in Florida, Angie had determined that they had to stay at Frampton Ranch and Resort and film at the History Tree.

Maura had suggested other places that would make great content for a book on the bizarre: sinkholes, a road where cars slid uphill instead of downhill—hell, she would have done her best to make a giant ball of twine sound fascinating. There were lots of other places in the state with strange stories—lord! They could go back to Key West and film a piece on Carl Tanzler, who had slept with the corpse of his beloved, Elena de Hoyos, for seven years.

But Angie was dead set on seeing the History Tree, and when they'd gotten to the clearing she had started spinning around like a delighted child.

She stopped suddenly, staring at Maura.

"You really are uncomfortable here, aren't you? Scared? You know, I've told you—you can hire an assistant. Maybe a strapping fellow, tall, dark and handsome—or blond and handsome—and muscle-bound. Someone to protect us if the bogeyman is around at any of our strange sites." Angie paused, grinning. She liked men and didn't apologize for it. In her own words, if you didn't kiss a bunch of frogs, you were never going to find a prince.

"Angie, I like doing my own work—and editing it and assuring that I like what I've done. I promise you, if we turn something into any kind of a feature film, we'll hire dozens of people."

Angie sighed. "Well, so much for tall, dark—or blond—and handsome. Your loss, my dear friend. Anyway. You do amazing work for me. You're a one-woman godsend."

"Thanks," Maura told her. She inhaled a deep breath.

"Could you try not to look quite so miserable?"

"Oh, Angie. I'm sorry. It's just..."

"The legend. The legend about the tree—oh, yes. And the murder victims found here. I'm sorry, Maura, but... I mean, I film these places because they have legends attached to them." Angie seemed to be perplexed. She sighed. "Of course, the one murder was just twelve years ago. Does that bother you?" Staring at

Maura, she gasped suddenly. "You're close to this somehow, right? Oh, my God! Were you one of the kids working here *that* summer? I mean, I'd have had no idea... You're from West Palm Beach. There's so much stuff down there. Ah!" It seemed that Angie didn't really need answers. "You wound up going to the University of Central Florida. You were near here..."

"Yes, I was here working that summer," Maura said flatly.

"Your name was never in the paper?"

"That's right. The police were careful to keep the employees away from the media. And since we are so isolated on the ranch, news reporters didn't get wind of anything until the next day. My parents had me out of here by then, and Donald Glass was emphatic about the press leaving his young staff alone."

"But a kid was *arrested*—"

"And released. And honestly, Angie, I am a little worried. Even if it has nothing to do with the past, there's something not good going on now. Haven't you watched the news? They found the remains of a young woman not far from here."

"Not far from here, but not *here*," Angie said. "Hey," she said again, frowning with concern. "That can't have anything to do with anything—the Frampton ranch killer committed suicide, I thought."

"One of the cooks killed himself," Maura said. "Yes, but… I mean, he never had his day in court. Most people believed he killed Francine—he hated her. But a lot of people disliked her."

"But he killed himself."

"Yes. I wasn't here then. I did hear about it, of course."

Angie was pensive for a moment, and then she asked, "Maura, you don't think that the tree is…evil, do you?"

"*Trees*—a palm laced in with an oak. And no. I'm quite accustomed to the spooky and creepy, and we both know that places don't become evil, nor do things. But people can be wicked as hell—and they can feed off legends. I don't like being out here—not alone. There will be a campfire tonight with the history and ghost stories and the walk—we'll join that. I have waivers for whoever attends tonight."

"What if someone doesn't want to be filmed?" Angie asked anxiously. "You tell the story just as well as anyone else, right? And the camera loves you—a perfect, slinky blonde beauty with those enormous gray eyes of yours. Come on, you've told a few of the stories before. You can—"

"I cannot do a good video for you as a selfie," Maura said patiently.

"Right. I can film you telling the story," Angie said. "Just that part. And I can do it now—I think you said that the stories were told by the campfire, and then the historic walk began. I'll get you—right here and now—doing the story part of it. Oh, and you can include... Oh, God!" Angie said, her eyes widening. "You weren't just here—you saw the dead woman! The murdered woman... I mean, from this century. Francine Renault. And they arrested a kid, Brock McGovern, but he was innocent, and it was proved almost immediately, but then... Well, then, if the cook didn't do it, they never caught the killer!"

Maura kept her face impassive. Angie always wrote about old crimes that were unsolved—and why a place was naturally haunted after ghastly deeds had occurred there.

She did her homework, however. Angie probably knew more than Maura remembered.

She had loved the sad legend of the beautiful Gyselle, who had died so tragically for love. But, of course, she would have delved as deeply as possible into every event that had occurred at the ranch.

"Do they—do they tell that story at the campfire?" Angie asked.

Maura sighed. "Angie, I haven't been here since the night it happened. I was still young. My parents dragged me home immediately."

She was here now—and she could remember that night all too clearly. Coming to the tree, then realizing while denying it that a real body was hanging from it. That it was Francine Renault. That she had been hanged from a heavy branch, hanged by the neck, and that she dangled far above the ground, tongue bulging, face grotesque.

She remembered screaming...

And she remembered the police and how they had taken Brock away, frowning and massively confused, still tall and straight and almost regally dignified.

And she could remember that there were still those who speculated on his guilt or innocence—until dozens of people had spoken out, having seen him through the time when Francine might have been taken and killed. His arrest had really been ludicrous—a detective's desperate bid to silence the horror and outrage that was beginning to spread.

Brock's life had changed, and thus her life had changed.

Everything had changed.

Except for this spot.

She could even imagine that she was a kid again, that she could see Francine Renault, so macabre in death, barely believable, yet so real and tragic and terrifying as she dangled from the thick limb.

"Oh," Angie groaned, the one word drawn out long enough to be a sentence. "Now I know why you were against doing a video here!"

Angie had wanted the History Tree. And when she had started to grow curious regarding Maura's reluctance to head to the Frampton Ranch and Resort—especially since the resort was supposedly great and the expense of rooms went on Angie's bill—Maura had decided it was time to cave.

She hadn't wanted to give any explanations.

"Angie, it's in your book, and you sell great and your video channel is doing great, as well. It's fine. Really. But because they did recently find what seems to be the remains of a murder

victim near here, I do think we need to be careful. As in, stay out of these woods after dark."

"There is a big bad wolf. Was a big bad
wolf… But seriously, I'm not a criminologist
of any kind, but I'd say the killer back then
was making a point. Maybe the bones they
found belonged to someone who died of natural causes."

Angie wasn't stupid, but Maura was sure
that the look she gave her tiny friend at that
moment implied that she thought she was.

"Maybe," Angie said defensively.

"Angie, you don't rot in the dirt on purpose
and then wind up with your bones in a cache
of hotel laundry," Maura said.

"No, but, hey—there could be another explanation. Like a car accident. And whoever
hit her was terrified and ran—and then, sadly,
she just rotted."

"And wound up in hotel sheets?"

Maura asked incredulously. Angie couldn't
be serious.

"Okay, so that's a bit far-fetched."

"Angie, it's been reported that the remains
were found of a murder victim. Last I saw,
they were still seeking her identity, but they
said that she was killed."

"Well, they found bones, from what I understand. Anyway," Angie said, dusting her hands on her skirt and speaking softly and with dignity and compassion, "I wish you would have just said that you were here when it happened. Let's get out of here. I'm sorry I made you do this."

"You didn't make me do it. If I had been determined not to come back here, I wouldn't have done so. But it's going to get dark soon. Let me shoot a bit of you doing your speech by the tree while I still have good light."

Maura lifted her camera, looked at the tree and then up at the sky.

They wouldn't have the light much longer.

"Angie, come on—let's film you."

"Please—you know the stories so well. Let me film you this time."

"They're your books."

"But you'll give me a great authenticity. I'll interview you—and you were here when the last crime occurred. I'm surprised they haven't hacked this sucker to the ground, really," Angie said, looking at the tree. "Or at the very least, they should have video surveillance out here."

"Now, that would be the right idea. They

have video surveillance in the lobby, the elevators—and other areas. But for now, please?"

They were never going to be able to leave.

"All right, all right!" Maura said. She adjusted the camera on its lightweight tripod and looked at the image on the camera's viewing screen. "I've got it lined up already. I'll go right there. You need to get it rolling. The mic is on already, and you can see what you're filming."

"Hey, I've used it before—not a lot, but I kind of know what I'm doing," Angie reminded her.

Maura stepped away from the camera and headed over to the tree. Angie had paid attention to her. She lifted her fingers and said, "In three…" and then went silent, counting down the rest by hand.

Maura was amazed at how quickly it all came back to her. She told the tale of the beautiful Gyselle and then went into the later crimes.

Ending, of course, with the murder of Francine Renault.

"A false lead caused the arrest of an innocent young man. But this is America, and we all know that any man is innocent until proved guilty, and this young man was quickly proved innocent. He was only under arrest for a night, because eyewitness reports confirmed he was with several other people—busy at work— when the crime took place. Still, it was a travesty, shattering a great deal of the promise of the young man's life. He was, however, as I said, quickly released—and until this day, the crime goes unsolved."

She finished speaking and saw that Angie was still running the camera, looking past her, appearing perplexed—and pleased—by something that she saw.

"Hello there! Are you with Frampton Ranch and Resort? You aren't, by any chance, the host for the campfire stories tonight, are you?"

Angie was smiling sweetly—having shifted into her flirtatious mode.

Curious, Maura turned around and started toward the path.

If a jaw could actually drop, hers did.

She quickly closed her mouth, but perhaps her eyes were bulging, as well. It seemed almost as if someone had physically knocked the breath from her.

Brock McGovern was standing there.

Different.

The same.

A bit taller than he'd been at eighteen; his shoulders had filled out and he appeared to have acquired a great deal more solid muscle. He filled out a dark blue suit and tailored shirt exceptionally well.

His face was the same...

Different.

There was something hard about him now that hadn't been there before. His features were leaner, his eyes...

Still deep brown. But they were harder now, too, or appeared to be harder, as if there was a shield of glass on them. He'd always walked and moved with purpose, confident in what he wanted and where he was going.

Now, just standing still, he was an imposing presence.

And though Angie had spoken, he was looking at Maura.

"Wow," Angie said softly. "Did I dream up the perfect assistant for you—tall, dark and to die for? Who the hell... The storyteller guy is wickedly cute, but this guy..."

He couldn't have heard her words; he wasn't close enough.

And he wasn't looking at her. He was staring at Maura.

"That was great," he said smoothly. "However, I don't consider my life to have been *shattered*. I mean—I hope I have fulfilled a few of the promises I made to myself."

Maura wanted to speak. Her mouth wouldn't work.

Angie, however, had no problem.

"Oh, my God!" Angie cried.

Every once in a while, her Valley girl came out.

"You—you're Brock McGovern?" she asked.

"I am," he said, but he still wasn't looking at Angie. He was locked on Maura. Then he smiled. A rueful smile, dry and maybe even a little bitter.

"Here—in Florida," Angie said. "I mean— at the History Tree."

He turned at last to face Angie. "I'm here for an investigation now. I'm going to suggest that you two head back to the resort and don't wander off alone. A woman's remains were found at a laundry facility not far from here, and there are three young women who have gone missing recently. Best to stay in the main areas—with plenty of people around."

"Oh!" Angie went into damsel-in-distress mode then. "Is it really dangerous, do you think? I'm so glad that you're here, if there is danger. I mean, we've seen the news…heard things, but seriously, bad things aren't necessarily happening here, right? It's just a tree. Florida is far from crime-free, but… Anyway, thank God that you're here. We didn't really think we needed to be afraid, but now you're here…and thank God! Right, Maura?"

Maura didn't reply. She'd heard Angie speaking as if she'd been far, far away. Then she found her voice. Or, at least, a whisper of it.

"Brock," she murmured.

"Maura," he returned casually. "Good to see you. Well, surprised to see you—but good to see you."

"Investigation," she said, grasping for something to say. She seemed to be able to manage one word at a time.

"I just told you—they found a woman's remains, and three young women who have been reported missing had a connection to the Frampton Ranch and Resort. The FDLE has asked for Bureau help," he explained politely.

"Yes, we were just talking about the young woman's remains—and the missing girls. I, uh, I think I'd heard that you did go into the FBI," she said. "And they sent you…here." There.

She had spoken in complete sentences. More or less. She'd been almost comprehensible.

"Yes, pretty much followed my original plans. Navy, college, the academy—FBI. And yes, I'm back here. Nothing like sending in an agent who knows the terrain," he said. "Shall we head back? I am serious. You shouldn't be in the woods alone when…well, when no one has any idea of what is really going on. We're not trying to incite fear. We're just trying to get a grip on what is happening, but I do suggest caution. Shall we head back?"

He was the same.

He was different.

And she was afraid to come too close to him. Afraid that the emotions of a teenager would erupt within her again, as if the years meant nothing…

If she got too close, she would either want to beat upon him, slamming her fists against his chest, demanding to know why he had never called, never tried to reach her and how it had been so easy to forget her.

Either that, or she would throw herself into his arms and sob and do anything just to touch him again.

Chapter Two

"The soil—clay based, some sand—like that covers most of the north of the state," Rachel Lawrence said.

She was seated across from Brock with Michael Flannery in the Java Bar on the Frampton property.

Rachel had changed. Her nails were cut short, clean of any color. Her hair was shorter, too. She still wore bangs, but her dark tresses were attractively trimmed to slide in angles along her face.

Everything about her appearance was serviceable. The girl who had once cried over a broken nail or scuffed sneakers had made an about-face.

She had greeted Brock politely and gravely, and seemed—like Flannery—to be anxious to have him working on the case with them.

"There's the beginning of a task force rumbling around," she'd told him when they'd first met in the coffee bar. "I'm lucky to be working with Michael Flannery—very lucky. But at this moment, while our superiors are listening, and they were willing to accept FBI involvement, they don't necessarily all believe that we are looking at a serial killer and this situation is about to blow up and get out of hand. It's great to have another officer who knows the lay of the land, so to speak."

"Yes, I do know it. And I've got to say, Rachel, I'm happy to see that you are working for the FDLE—and that you're so pleased to be where you are."

She made a face. "Oh, well, there was a time when I thought I wanted to be rich and elite, own a teacup Yorkie in a designer handbag and be supported in fine fashion. But I do love what I do. Oh—I actually do have a teacup Yorkie. Love the little guy!"

It had been far easier to meet back up with Rachel—and even Nils and Mark Hartford—than Brock had expected.

Time.

It healed all wounds, right?

Wrong. Why not? He believed he was, as

far as any normal psychology went, long over what had happened regarding his arrest for murder at such a young age—he'd barely been in jail before his parents arrived with their attorney, his dad so indignant that the icy chill in his eyes might have gotten Brock released before the attorney even opened his mouth.

Truly, he had seen and heard far worse in the navy. And, God knew, some of the cases he'd handled as an agent in a criminal investigation unit had certainly been enough to chill the blood.

Still...the haunting memories regarding the forest and the History Tree clung to him like the moss that dripped from the old oaks.

"A Yorkie, huh?" he asked Rachel, remembering that she was there.

They both grinned, and he assured her that he liked dogs, all dogs, and didn't have one himself only because it wouldn't be fair to the animal—he was always working.

Rachel went on with the information—or lack of it—that she had worked to obtain.

"Some of our elegant hotels have special bedding, but...lots don't. The sheets around the remains might have come from five different chain hotels that cover North Florida, Central

Florida and the Panhandle, all of which have twenty to forty local franchises. That means that Maureen Rodriguez might have been murdered anywhere in all that area—buried first nearby or somewhere different within the boundaries—and then dug up and wrapped in sheets."

"You checked with the truck drivers making deliveries that day, naturally?" Brock asked her.

She gave him a look that was both amused and withering. "I did go to college—and I majored in criminology. I'm not just a piece of fluff, you know."

Detective Michael Flannery grunted. "She's tailing me—I'm teaching her everything I know. And," he added, "how not to make the same mistakes."

Brock nodded his appreciation for the comment and asked, "Were you able to narrow it down by the drivers and their deliveries?"

"The way it works is that they pick up when they drop off," Rachel said. "So it's not as if they're kept separately. It's almost like recycling receptacles—the hotels have these massive canvas bags. The sheets are all the same, so they drop off dirty and pick up clean replacements. The laundry is also responsible for getting rid of sheets that are too worn, too stained, too whatever. But the driver drop-offs do narrow it down to hotels from St. Augustine to Gainesville and down to northern Ocala. I have a list of them, which I've emailed and..." She paused, reaching into her bag for a small folder that she presented to Brock. "Here—hard copy."

He looked at the list. There were at least thirty hotels with their addresses listed.

"All right, thank you," he told her. "I'd like to start by talking to Katie Simmons—the woman who reported Lydia Merkel missing. And then the last person to see each of the missing young women."

"Cops have interviewed all of them. I saw Katie Simmons myself," Flannery told him. "I'm not sure what else you can get from her."

"Humor me. And this list—I'd like you to get state officers out with images of all the women. Let's see what they get—they'll tell us if they find anyone who has seen any of them or thinks they might have seen someone like them. We need the images plastered everywhere—a Good Samaritan could call in and let us know if they saw one of the women walking on the street, buying gas…at a bar or a restaurant."

"The images have been broadcast," Flannery said. "I asked for you, but come on. We're not a bunch of dumb hicks down here, you know."

Brock grinned. "I'm a Fed, remember?"

Flannery shrugged. "You're a conch," he reminded Brock, referring to the moniker given to Key West natives.

"I get you, but I'm not referring to local news. I mean, we need likenesses of the young women—all four of them—out everywhere. We need to draw on media across the state and beyond. And we need to get them up in all the colleges—there are several of them in the area. All four of the women were college age—they might have friends just about anywhere. They might have met up with someone at a party."

"I'll get officers on the hotels and take the colleges with Rachel. She and I can head in opposite directions and cover more ground." Flannery hesitated. "I've arranged for us to see the ME first thing, so we'll start all else after that—I assumed you wanted to see the remains of Maureen Rodriguez."

"Yes, and thank you," Brock told him. "Do I meet you at the morgue?"

"No, we'll head out together—if that's all right with you. I have a room here and so does Rachel. I'm setting mine up as a headquarters," Flannery said. "I'll start a whiteboard—that way, we can keep up with any information any of us acquires and have it in plain sight, as we'd be doing if we were running the investigation out of one of our offices."

"A good plan," Brock said. "But tomorrow I would like to get started over in St. Augustine as quickly as possible."

"All right, then. We will take two cars tomorrow morning. Compare notes back here, say, late afternoon. Get in touch sooner if we have something that seems of real significance. It's good that you decided to be based here. Easier than trying to come and go."

Flannery hesitated, looking at Brock. Then he shrugged. "Mr. Glass actually came to me." He lowered his voice, even though there was no one near them. "On the hush-hush. Said his wife didn't even know. Seems he's afraid himself that someone is using this place or the legends that go with it."

Brock drained his cup of coffee. "Can you set me up with Katie Simmons for some time tomorrow?" he asked Rachel.

"Yes, sir, I can and will," she assured him. "She's in St. Augustine."

Brock stood.

They looked up at him.

"And now?" Flannery asked.

"You wanted me here because I know the place," Brock said. "I'm going to watch a couple of the people that I knew when I worked here. See what's changed—and who has changed and how. I'm not leaving the property tonight. If there's anything, call me. And I'll check in later."

"You're going to the campfire tales and ghost walk?" Flannery asked.

"Not exactly—but kind of," Brock said. He nodded to the two of them and headed out, glancing at his watch.

He did know the place, that was certain. Almost nothing on the grounds had changed.

His father had heard about the place—that it was a great venue for young people to work for the summer during high school. There was basic housing for them, a section of rooms for girls and one for boys. They weren't allowed off the grounds unless they had turned eighteen or they were supervised; any dereliction of the rules called for immediate dismissal.

The positions were highly prized—if anyone broke the rules, they were damned careful not to be caught.

Of course, fraternizing—as in sex—had not been in the rules.

Kids were kids.

But with him and Maura…

It had felt like something more than kids being kids.

He still believed it. He wondered if, just somewhere in her mind, she believed it, too.

MARK HARTFORD PROVED to be excellent at telling the stories—despite the fact that he'd told Maura that he was afraid that night. Well, not afraid but nervous.

"You were so good!" he had said to Maura when he saw that she and Angie were going to be in his audience. "So good!"

He'd been just about fourteen when she knew him years before; he had to be about twenty-five or twenty-six now. He'd grown up, of course, and he still charmed with a boyish energy and enthusiasm that was contagious. His eyes were bright blue and his hair—just slightly shaggy—was a tawny blond. He'd grown several inches since Maura had seen him, and he evidently made use of the resort's gym.

Angie was entranced by Mark. But she'd always been unabashed about her appreciation of men in general—especially when they were attractive. Maura didn't consider herself to be particularly suspicious of the world in general, but she did find that she often felt much older and wiser when she was with Angie—warning her that it wasn't always good to be quite so friendly with every good-looking man that she met.

"I'm sure you're just as good a storyteller," Angie had told Mark.

"I try—I have a lot to live up to," he'd said in return, answering Angie, smiling from one of them to the other.

Maura was somewhat pleased by the distraction. Angie had been talking incessantly about Brock and she'd finally stopped—long enough to do a new assessment of Mark Hartford.

She had decided that she liked young Mark Hartford very much, as well.

They'd already seen Nils in the restaurant. Mark and Nils were easily identifiable as brothers, but Mark's evident curiosity and sincere interest in everyone and everything around him made him the more naturally charming of the two.

"Ooh, I do like both brothers. But the other guy...the FBI guy... Hey, he was the one they arrested—and he turned out to be FBI! Cool. I appreciate them all, but that Brock guy...sexier—way sexier," Angie had said.

Actually, Maura found Angie's honesty one of the nicest things about her. She said what she was thinking or feeling pretty much all the time.

Now the tales were underway. Mark was telling them well. Maura allowed herself to survey his audience.

There were—as there had always been, so it seemed—a group of young teens, some together, some with their parents. There were couples, wives or girlfriends hanging on to their men, and sometimes a great guy admittedly frightened by the dark and tales and hanging on to his girlfriend or wife or boyfriend or husband, as well. There were young men and women, older men and women—a group of about twenty-five or thirty in all.

She couldn't help but remember how her group had been about the same size that night twelve years ago—and how they had all reacted when they reached the History Tree.

She had screamed—so had several people.

Some had laughed—certain that the swinging body was a prop and perhaps part of a gag set up by the establishment to throw a bit of real scare into the evening.

And then had come the frantic 911 calls, the horror as everyone realized that the dead woman was real and Brock trying to herd people away and, even then, trying to see that the scene wasn't trampled, that as a crime scene it wasn't disturbed…

Only to be arrested himself.

Tonight, Maura had her camera; she also had waivers signed by everyone in the group. She'd been lucky that night—everyone had been happy to meet her and Angie—and they all wanted their fifteen minutes of fame. They were fine with being on camera with Angie Parsons.

They were still by the campfire.

She was thinking about Brock.

Determining how much she was going to video after Mark's speech, she looked across the campfire to the place where the trees edged around the fire and the storyteller and his audience.

Brock was leaning against a tree, arms crossed over his chest, listening.

He was no longer wearing a suit; he was in jeans and a plaid flannel shirt—he could pass himself off as a logger or such. Her heart seemed to do a little leap and she was angry at herself, angry that she could still find him so compellingly attractive.

Twelve years between them. Not a word. They weren't even friends on social media.

He must have sensed her looking at him. She realized that his gaze had changed direction; he was looking at her across the distance.

He nodded slightly and then frowned, shaking his head.

He didn't want to be on camera; she nodded.

She turned away, dismissing him.

She tried to focus on the words that Mark Hartford was saying.

The stories were the same. Until they came to the History Tree.

There, a new story had been added in. Mark talked about the tour that had come upon Francine Renault.

He wasn't overly dramatic; he told the facts,

and admitted that, yes, he had been among those who had found her.

The story ended with the death of the cook, Peter Moore, who had stabbed himself and been found in the freezer, his favorite knife protruding from his chest.

A fight had gone too far, or so the authorities believed, and Moore had killed Francine. And then later, in remorse or fear that prison would be worse than death, he had committed suicide.

On that tragic note, the story of the History Tree ended. As did the nightly tour.

Mark then told his group that they needed to head back—there had been some trouble in the area lately and the management would appreciate it if guests refrained from being in the forest at night and suggested that no one wander the woods alone.

As they began to filter back, Maura saw that Brock didn't go with the others.

She might have been the only one to note his presence; he had apparently followed silently at a bit of a distance, always staying back within the trees.

She turned when the group left. As they headed back along the trail, Brock stepped from his silent watching spot in the darkness of the surrounding foliage. He walked to the History Tree.

He stood silently, staring up at it, as if seeking some answer there.

Mark was asking if the tourists wanted coffee or tea or a drink before they called it a night.

Angie had already said yes.

Maura turned away from Brock purposefully and followed Angie and Mark. Once they reached the lodge, she would beg off.

All she wanted to do that night was crawl into a hole somewhere and black out.

Her room and her bed would have to do—even if she didn't black out and lay awake for hours, ever more furious with herself that she was allowing herself to feel...

Anything about him. Anything at all.

"I've seen some strange things in my day," Rita Morgan, the medical examiner, said. She was a tall, lean woman, looked to be about forty-five and certainly the no-nonsense type.

"Many a strange thing, and some not so strange. Too many bodies out of the ocean and the rivers, a few in barrels, some sunk with cement." She pursed her lips, shaking her head. "This one? Strange and sad. As long as I've done this, been an ME, it still never ceases to amaze me—man's inhumanity to fellow man." She looked up at Brock and Flannery and shook her head again. "Thing that saves me is when I see a young person get up and help the disabled or the elderly—then I get to know that there's as much good out there as bad—more, hopefully. Yeah, yeah, that doesn't help you any. I just… Well, I can show you the remains. I can't tell you too much about them. No stomach content—no stomach. I had disarticulated bones with small amounts of flesh still attached—and a skull."

She stepped back to display the gurney that held the remains of a young woman's life, tragically—and brutally—cut short.

"It looks as if she was killed a long time ago—but from my brief, she was only missing about three months," Brock said, looking from Flannery to the medical examiner.

And then to the table.

Bits of hair and scalp still adhered to the skull.

"Decomposition is one of those things that can vary incredibly. I believe she was killed approximately two months ago. Particular to situations like this, the internal organs began to deteriorate twenty-four to seventy-two hours after death. The number of bacteria and insects in the area have an effect on the outer body and soft tissue. Three to five days—you have bloating. Within ten days, insects, the elements and bacteria have been busy and you have massive accumulations of gas. Within a few weeks, nails and teeth begin to go. After a month, the body becomes fluid."

"The skull retains a mouthful of teeth," Brock noted.

"Yes, which is why I believe decomp had the best possible circumstances. Lots of earth—and water. Rain, maybe. Even flooding in the area where the body was first left. As I said, there's no way to pinpoint an exact time of death. It's approximately two months' time. I also believe, per decomp, that she was left out in the elements—maybe a bit of dirt and some leaves were shoveled over her. It's been a warm winter, and the soil here can be rich—and as we all know, this is Florida. We have plenty of insects.

"The question is, after all that decomp in the wild, how in the world did she come to be in sheets at an industrial laundry? But that's your problem. Mine is cause of death. Not much to go on, as you can see, but enough." She pointed with a gloved hand. "That rib bone. You can see. The scraping there wasn't any insect—that was caused by a sharp blade. There's a second such mark on that rib—would have been the other side of the rear rib cage. In my educated estimation, she was stabbed to death. Without more tissue or organs I can't tell you how many wounds she sustained—exactly how many times she was stabbed—but I do imagine the attack would have been brutal, and that she probably suffered mortal damage to many of her organs. There's no damage to the skull."

"Were there any defensive wounds you were able to find on the arm bones?" Brock asked.

Flannery was standing back, letting Brock ask his own questions, since the detective had already seen the remains and spoken with the ME earlier.

"No, there were no defensive wounds, Special Agent McGovern," Dr. Morgan said. "She was stabbed from behind. She might never have seen her killer. Or she might have trusted him—or her. It was violent assault, I can tell you that. But—I am assuming that she didn't want to be stabbed to death—she had to have been taken by surprise. She never had a chance to fight back at all. Some of what I've been saying I'm assuming, but I am making assumptions based on education and experience. I'm the ME—you guys are the detectives. Can't help having an opinion."

"Of course, that's fine, and thank you," Brock said. "The sheets are at the lab? Still being tested?"

"Yes. They can't pinpoint the sheets to a certain hotel because too many of them buy from the same supplier."

She covered the remains.

She looked at Brock curiously, studying him. Then she smiled broadly. "You came out all right, it seems." She glanced over at Flannery. "Despite what you did to him."

"Hey, I acted on the best info I had at the time," Flannery said.

"Rash—hey, he was a newbie at the time. Didn't know his—oh, never mind. But good to see you—as a law enforcement officer, Agent McGovern."

"Well, thank you. I'm sorry, did we meet before?" he asked her.

She shook her head. "I was new in this office. But I assisted at the autopsies for both Francine Renault and the cook, Peter Moore..." She left off, shrugging. "I knew that they'd brought you in—one of the summer kids. Because you were seen in some kind of major verbal altercation with her. And arrested, from what I understand, on a *tip*."

She didn't exactly sniff, but she did look at Detective Flannery with a bit of disdain.

"I say again, I acted on the best info I had at the time. And yeah—I guess he came out all right," Flannery said with something that sounded a bit like a growl in his voice. He eyed Brock, as if not entirely sure about him yet.

"I spent only one night in jail. Trust me, I spent many a worse night in the service," he assured Dr. Morgan and Flannery.

Flannery looked away, uncomfortable. Dr. Morgan smiled.

"Thank you," he told her. "If there's anything else that comes to mind that might be of any assistance whatsoever..."

"I'll be quicker than a rabbit in heat," she vowed solemnly.

He arched his brows slightly but managed a smile and another thank-you.

Brock and Flannery left the county morgue

together. They'd come in Flannery's official vehicle; it would allow them to bypass heavy traffic if needed, Flannery had said.

Brock preferred to drive himself, but that day, while Flannery drove, it gave him a chance to look through his notes on the victim.

"She stayed at the Frampton Ranch and Resort three months ago," he murmured out loud. "Her home was St. Pete. She wasn't reported missing right away because she was over eighteen and had been living alone in St. Augustine, working as a cocktail waitress—but hadn't shown up for work in over a week. Says here none of her coworkers really knew her—she had just started."

"The perfect victim," Flannery said. He glanced sideways at Brock. "The other missing girls... You have the information on them, too, right?"

"Yeah, I have it online and on paper. I have to hand it to Egan. He believes in hard copy and there are times it proves to be especially beneficial."

"And saves on eyestrain," Flannery muttered. He glanced Brock's way again. "You know, I asked for you specifically. Hope you don't mind too much. Can't help it. Still think there's something with that damned resort, even if I can't pin it. Well, I mean, back then, of course, it had to do with the ranch. Francine Renault worked there—and died there. But... that tree has seen a lot of death."

He said it oddly, almost as if he was in awe of the tree. Brock frowned, looking over at him. Flannery didn't glance his way, but apparently knew he was being studied.

"Well, bad stuff happens there," Flannery said.

"Right—because bad people like the aspect that bad things happened there."

"You think it should be chopped down."

"It might dissuade future killers."

"Or just cause them to leave their victims somewhere else," Flannery said. "Or create a new History Tree or haunted bog or...just a damnable stretch of roadway."

"True," Brock agreed.

"What drives me crazy is the why—I mean, we all study this stuff. Some killers are simply goal driven—they want or need someone out of the way. Some killings have to do with passion and anger and jealousy. Some have to do with money. Some people are psychotic and kill for the thrill or the sexual release it gives them. Years ago, it was just Francine. Now, that Francine—I didn't find a single soul who actually said they liked her, but it never seemed she'd done anything bad enough to make someone want to kill her. She seemed to be more of an annoyance—like a fly buzzing around your ear."

"Maybe she was a really, really annoying fly—buzzing at the wrong person," Brock said. Then he reminded the detective, "Peter Moore committed suicide. There was no note—but maybe he did do it, because he was afraid of being apprehended, or felt overwhelming remorse or was dealing with an untreated mental illness that led him down a very dark path. Seems to me that everyone accepted the fact that he must have done it—though he sure as hell didn't get his day in court."

Flannery glanced his way at last. "But you don't think that Peter Moore killed Francine any more than I do."

Brock hesitated and then said flatly, "No. And I knew Peter Moore. He hated Francine, but he held his own with her—he didn't really have to answer to her. He was directly under Fred Bentley. I don't think he killed Francine. I don't even think that Peter Moore killed himself."

Flannery nodded. "There you go—see? There was a reason I needed you down here. Damn, though, if it doesn't seem like home-coming somehow."

"What do you mean?"

"I mean, I can't just buy the theory that Peter Moore did it, either. In my mind, the killer might have helped him into that so-called sui-cide. No prints but Peter's on the knife in his gut, but hell, the kitchen is filled with gloves."

"So it is."

"That beauty is back, as well," Flannery said, glancing his way once again.

Brock didn't ask who Flannery meant. That was dead obvious. Maura.

"Did you ask her up here?" Brock asked him.

"Me?" Flannery was truly surprised. "I barely met her back in the day, and she was fairly rattled when I did... Well, you were there. You didn't ask for her to be here? I'd have thought, at least, that the two of you would still be friends. You were hot and heavy back then, so I heard—the beautiful young ones!"

"I hadn't seen her since that night until I saw her again late yesterday afternoon—out by the tree."

"Ah, yes, she's with that web queen or writer—or whatever that little woman calls herself," Flannery said. He looked over at Brock. "Is that what they call serendipity?"

Brock didn't reply. He was looking at his portfolios on the missing women. He'd already read through them on the plane, but talking things out could reveal new angles.

"All right," Brock said. "Maureen Rodriguez was out of the house and just starting a new life. So she wasn't noted as missing right away. But Lily Sylvester was supposed to check in with her boyfriend. She'd come to the Frampton ranch because she wanted to see it. She stayed at a little hotel on the outskirts of St. Augustine one night after her visit, and then she was supposed to meet with a girlfriend at a posh bed-and-breakfast in the old section of the city. She never showed that day and her friend called the cops right away."

He flipped through his folders.

"Friends and family were insistent about Lily," Flannery told him. "She was as dependable as they come. Is," he added. "We shouldn't assume the worst."

But it was natural that they did.

"All right, moving on to Amy Bonham. She

stayed at the Frampton ranch. She told one of the waitresses that she was excited about a surprise job opportunity the next day. She was supposed to be heading in the other direction—toward Orlando and the theme parks. She also stayed at a chain motel the night right after she was at the Frampton ranch and disappeared the next day. I know you certainly looked into her 'job opportunity.'"

Flannery nodded. "We've had officers interviewing people across more than half the state."

"But no one knew anything about it."

"No. But the waitress at the Frampton ranch—Dorothy Masterson—swears that Amy was super excited. Dorothy believed that she was looking for work at one of the theme parks."

"And you checked with all the parks."

"Of course. Big and small."

Brock went on to his third folder. "Lydia Merkel."

Flannery nodded; he'd already committed to memory most of what Brock was still studying.

"Lydia. Cute as a button."

"You met her? You knew her?" Brock asked, frowning.

"I met her briefly—I was in St. Augustine.

The wife had her nephews down and I was taking them on one of the ghost tours. Lydia was on our tour. All wide eyes and happiness. Can't tell you how stunned I was when the powers that be called me in and told me that we had another missing woman—and that I recognized her." He glanced quickly at Brock. "You know how it goes with missing persons reports. Half of the time someone is just off on a lark. There's been a fight—a person has taken off because they want to disappear. But I just don't think that's the case." He was silent. "Especially since we found the remains of Maureen Rodriguez."

"And you can't help but think that Frampton Ranch and Resort is somehow involved."

Flannery nodded grimly.

"Lydia had told a young woman she was working with—Katie Simmons—that she wanted to take her first days off to drive over and see the History Tree. We're not just working this alone. I have all kinds of help on this. We do have officers from the Florida Department of Law Enforcement out all over—not to mention the help we've gotten from our local police departments. I keep feeling like I'm looking at some kind of puzzle with pieces missing—except that the frame is there. Because there was only one thing the girls—or young women—had in common."

"They had left or were coming to the Frampton Ranch and Resort," Brock said.

He felt a sudden pang deep in his heart or maybe his soul—someplace that really hurt at any rate.

He glanced over at Flannery. "The four of them are between the ages of twenty-two and twenty-nine," he said.

"Lydia Merkel was—is—twenty-nine. She was at the ranch with friends for her birthday. On the tour, she talked about loving ghost stories—and how excited she was going to be to see the infamous History Tree."

Seriously—the tree should have been bulldozed.

Not fair—the tree wasn't guilty. Men and women could be guilty; the tree was just a tree—two trees.

"Funny, isn't it?" Flannery asked. "I mean, not ha ha funny, just…strange. Maybe ironic. The History Tree is two trees. Entwined. And you're here—because I asked for you particularly because I knew you were FBI, criminal section—and I'm here. And Miss Maura

Antrim is here. We're all kinds of entwined. And I can't help but think that we still know the killer—even if twelve years have gone by."

"Yep. We're all tangled together somehow, like that damned tree. And so help me God, this time I really want to have the answers… and to stop the killing," Brock said quietly.

"You don't disagree with me?" Flannery asked him.

Brock shrugged grimly.

"But you don't disagree—you don't think I'm being far-fetched or anything?" Flannery pressed.

"No, I just wonder what this person—if it is the same killer—has been doing for twelve years," Brock said. And then added, "Although…maybe he hasn't been lying dormant. It's a big state filled with just about everything in one area or another. Forests, marshes, caverns, sinkholes, the Everglades—a river of grass—and, of course…"

"That great big old Atlantic Ocean," Flannery said. "So, there you go. My puzzle. Are there pieces missing? Did the three young ladies who disappeared just run off? Or…"

"Has someone been killing young women and disposing of corpses over the last twelve years?" Brock finished. He took a deep breath. "All right, I guess I'm going to do a lot of traveling. There will be dozens of people to question again. But I think I'll start at the library at Frampton ranch."

ANGIE WAS A late sleeper, something Maura deeply appreciated the next morning. She wanted some on-her-own time.

She had gotten a lot of great footage for Angie's internet channel on the tour the night before.

Martin had ended up loving being on camera—and it had loved him. They were going to do the campfire again that night, get more video and put together all the best parts.

She'd behaved perfectly normally, even though she was ready to crawl out of her own skin. While on the tour, she'd expected to see Brock materialize again.

It hadn't been until the very end that she'd realized he'd been there all along—watching from the shadows, from the background.

But he'd never approached her. She'd seen him later in the lounge, briefly, when she and Angie walked in after the trek through the woods. He'd been deep in conversation with a slightly older man in a suit—she'd seen him earlier and remembered him vaguely. He was a cop of some kind; he'd been there the night that Francine Renault was killed. She had seen him earlier in the day as well, walking around the ranch with a woman. Maura hadn't seen the woman's face, just the cut of her suit, and for some bizarre reason she had noticed the woman's shoes. Flat, serviceable.

And she'd thought that perhaps the woman was a cop or in some form of law enforcement, too.

Angie hadn't seemed interested in talking to any of them—Maura had been glad. She'd left Angie in the lounge, waiting for her appointed drink with Mark, and Maura had slipped quickly upstairs, wanting nothing more than to be in her room, alone.

Once there, she'd lain awake for hours, wondering why something that had happened ages ago still had such an effect on her life—on her.

Why... Brock McGovern could suddenly walk back into her life and become all that she thought about once again. So easily. Or why she could close her eyes and see the man he had become and know that he was still somehow flawed and perfect, the man to whom she had subconsciously—or even consciously—compared to everyone else she ever met.

He hadn't so much as touched her.

And he hadn't looked at her as if he particularly liked her. He'd simply wanted her—and Angie—to be safe. Nothing more. Stay with people. He was a law enforcement officer, a Fed. He worked to find those who had turned living, breathing bodies into murdered, decaying bodies—and he tried to keep all men and women from being victims. His job. What he did.

A job he always knew he wanted.

She had to stop thinking about him, and that meant she needed to immerse herself in some other activity—research. Books, knowledge, seeking...

She had always loved the library and archives at the Frampton ranch. One thing Donald Glass did with every property he bought was build and maintain a library with any books and info he had on that property. It was fascinating—much of it had been put on computer through the years, but every little event that had to do with the property was available.

The hotel manager—solid, ruddy little Fred

Bentley—had never shown any interest in the contents of the library.

Nor, when she'd been alive, had Francine Renault. But the libraries were sacred. No matter what else the very, very rich Donald Glass might be, he loved his history and his libraries, and anyone working for him learned not to mess with them.

For this, she greatly admired Glass. Not that she knew the man well—he'd left the hands-on management to Francine and Fred when Maura had been working there. And back then, she and Brock had both spent hours in the library—often together—each trying to one-up the other by finding some obscure and curious fact or happening. It was fun to work the weird trivia into their presentations.

That had been twelve years ago.

But Brock was suddenly back in her life.

No, he wasn't in her life. He just happened to be here at the same time.

Because a woman had been murdered—and others had disappeared.

Concentrate... There was a wealth of information before her. Bits and pieces that might offer up something especially unusual for Angie Parsons.

The library room was comfortable and inviting, filled with leather sofas and chairs, desks, computers—and shelves upon shelves of files and books.

Donald Glass had acquired an extensive collection; he had books on the indigenous population of the area, starting back somewhere between twelve and twenty thousand years ago. Settlers had arrived before the end of the Pleistocene megafauna era. The Wacissa River—not far away in Jefferson County near the little town of Wacissa—had offered up several animal fossils of the time, and other areas of the state—including Silver Springs, Vero, Melbourne and Devil's Den—had also offered up proof of man's earliest time in the area.

Way back that many thousands of years, there had been a greater landmass and less water, causing animals—and thus hunters—to congregate at pools. Artifacts proving the existence of these hunter-gatherers could be found in countless rivers—and even out into the Gulf of Mexico.

Mammoths had even roamed the state.

By 700 AD, farming had come to the north of Florida. There were many Native American tribes, and many of those were called Creek by the Europeans and spoke the Muskogee language. But by the time the first Frampton put down roots to create this great ranching and farming estate, Florida Indians of many varieties—though mostly Creek—were being lumped together as Seminoles, largely divided into two groups: the Muskogee-speaking and the Hitchiti-speaking.

There were wonderful illustrated books describing fossils and tools found, creating images of the people and the way they lived.

According to the one she pulled from the shelf there had been a colony of Seminole living in the area when Frampton first chose his site.

They had held rites out at what was already a giant clearing in the forest. It was the Native Americans who had first called it the History Tree. The Timucua had first named it so; the Seminoles in the area had respected the holiness of the tree.

Maura—like the writer of the book—didn't believe that the Native American tribes had practiced human sacrifice at the tree. But as war loomed with the Seminole tribe, the European populace had liked to portray the native people as barbarians—it made it easier to justify killing them.

So the tree had gotten its reputation very early on.

Gyselle—who became known as Gyselle Frampton, since no one knew her real surname—had arrived at the plantation soon after it was built in the late 1830s. Spanish missionaries had "rescued" her from the Seminole, but she was fifteen at the time and had been kidnapped at the age of ten—or that was the best that could be figured. Oliver Frampton—creator of the first great mansion to rest on the property—had been a kind man. He'd taken her in, clothed her, educated her and had still, of course, given her chores to do.

She was a servant and not of the elite. She was not, in any way, wife material for his son.

That hadn't stopped Richard Frampton from falling in love with his father's beautiful servant/ward.

But Richard had underestimated his wife. Back then, a wife was supposed to be a lovely figurehead, wealthy to match her husband and eye candy on the arm of her man. Unless she was very, very, very rich—and then it wouldn't matter if she was eye candy or not.

But Julie LeBlanc Frampton had been no fool and not someone to be taken lightly.

She discovered the affair—and knew that her husband loved Gyselle deeply. Perhaps she was angry with her father-in-law for not only condoning the affair but perhaps finding it to be fine and natural. Wives weren't supposed to get in the way of these things after all.

Or maybe the situation was just convenient for her plan.

She hid the taste of the deadly fruit of the manchineel tree in a drink—one that Gyselle usually made up for the senior Mr. Frampton right before he went to bed made up of whiskey, tea and sugar.

The old man died in horrible pain. Julie immediately pointed the finger at Gyselle.

She created such an outcry and hysteria that the other servants immediately went for poor Gyselle. The master had been well loved. And without trial or even much questioning, they had dragged Gyselle out to the History Tree— thought to surely be haunted at that time and also a place where the devil might well be found.

Gyselle died swearing that she was innocent—and cursing Julie, those around her and even the tree.

After she was hanged, she was allowed to remain there until she rotted, until her bones fell to the ground.

Three years later, Julie Frampton died. At the time no one knew what her ailment was—tuberculosis, it sounded like to Maura.

But in the end, the true poisoner did die choking on her own blood—and confessing to the entire room that she had murdered her father-in-law.

"Maura!"

She had become so involved in what she was reading that the sound of her name made her jump.

She'd been very comfortable in one of the plush leather chairs, feet curled beneath her, the book—*Truth and Legends of Central Florida*—in her arms.

Luckily, she didn't drop it or throw it as she was startled. It was an original book, printed and bound in 1880.

"Mr. Glass!" she exclaimed, truly started to see the resort's owner. He usually kept to himself; Fred Bentley was his mouthpiece.

She quickly closed the book and stood, accepting the hand he offered to her.

Donald Glass, in his early sixties now, Maura thought, was still an attractive man. He kept himself lean and fit—and had maintained a full head of salt-and-pepper hair. His posture was straight; his manners tended to be impeccable. He'd never personally fired anyone that she knew of, in any of his enterprises. He left managers—like Fred Bentley—to do such deeds. He was customarily well liked and treated kindly by magazines when he was included in an article.

Donald Glass used his money to make more money, granted. That was the American way. But he did it all in one of the best possible manners—preserving history and donating to worthy causes all the while.

Whether he was into the causes or simply into tax breaks, no one really looked too closely.

But he tended to do good things and do them well.

"Miss Antrim, how lovely to have you here again," he said, smiling. "And I'm delighted that you've brought Angie Parsons with her incredible ability to show the world interesting places—and provide wonderful publicity for those places!"

"I'd love to take the credit, Mr. Glass," Maura told him. "Angie heard the story about the History Tree. She couldn't wait to come."

"Well, however you came to be here, I'm most delighted. Still sorry—and I will be sorry all my life—about Francine. She was…"

He paused. Maura wondered what he'd been about to say. That Francine Renault had been a good woman? But she really hadn't been kind or generous in any way.

"No one deserved to die that way," he said. "Anyway… I did consider having the tree torn out of the ground. But I thought on it a long time and decided that it was the *History Tree*. They didn't burn down the building when a famous woman died in a room at the Hard Rock in Hollywood, Florida, and…" Again, he paused. "I decided that the tree—or trees— should stay. Not to mention the fact that the environmentalists and preservationists would create a real uproar if we were to cut it down. It's hundreds of years old, you know. And yes—as you learned last night, we do tell the story at the campfire and continue the walk by the tree."

"Trees aren't evil," Maura said.

She wondered if she was trying to reassure him—or if it was something she said but doubted somewhere in a primal section of her heart or mind.

"No, of course not. A tree is a tree. Or trees are trees," he said and smiled weakly. "Anyway, I'm delighted to see you. And thankful for the work you're doing here with Miss Parsons."

"I'm not sure you need us. You've always had a full house here."

He didn't argue.

"I'm sure Marie will be delighted to see you, too."

"A pleasure to see her," Maura murmured.

Marie was perhaps ten years younger than her husband; they had been together for thirty years or so. Like her husband she kept herself fit, and she was an attractive and cordial woman. Her public manner was pristine—every once in a while, Maura had wondered what she was *really* thinking.

Glass lifted a hand in farewell and said, "Enjoy your stay." He started to walk away and then turned back. "I don't mean to be an alarmist, but...be careful. I'm sure you heard. Remains were found nearby. And several young women have disappeared, as well. Whether they ran away or…met with bad things… I know you're smart, but…be wary."

"Yes, I've heard. And I'll be careful," Maura said.

She watched him for a moment as he headed out of the room and then she opened the book again. Words swam before her as she tried to remember where she'd left off.

She heard Glass speaking again and she looked toward the door, thinking that he had something else to say.

But he wasn't speaking to her.

Brock was at the doorway, his tone deep and quiet as he replied to whatever Glass had said.

The length of Maura's body gripped with tension, which angered her to no end.

She hadn't seen or heard from him in twelve years.

He and Glass parted politely.

Brock headed straight for her. He smiled, but it seemed that his smile was grave.

His face seemed harder than the image of him she'd held in her mind. Naturally. Years did that to anyone.

And he'd always wanted to be law enforcement. But that job had to take a toll.

"I thought I'd find you here," he said softly.

"Yes, well, I... I'm here," she said.

She didn't invite him to sit. He did anyway. She wondered if he was going to talk about the years between them, ask what she'd been doing, maybe even explain why he'd just disappeared after the charges against him had been dismissed.

Elbows on his knees, hands folded idly, he was close—too close, she thought. Or not really close at all. Just close because she could feel a strange rush inside, as if she knew everything about him, or everything that mattered. She knew his scent—his scent, not soap or aftershave or cologne, but that which lurked beneath it, particular to him, something that drew her to him, that called up a natural reaction within her. She knew that there was a small scar on the lower side of his abdomen—stitches from a deep cut received when he'd fallen on a haphazardly discarded tin can during a track event when he'd been in high school. She knew there was a spattering of freckles on his shoulders, knew...

"You really shouldn't be here—you need to pack up and go," he said. His tone was harsh, as if she were committing a grave sin by being there.

She couldn't have been more surprised if he'd slapped her.

"I beg your pardon?" she demanded, a sudden fury taking over.

"You need to get the hell out—out of this part of the state and sure as hell off the Frampton Ranch and Resort."

Why did it hurt so badly, the way he spoke to her, the way he wanted to be rid of her?

"I'm sorry. I have every right to be here. It's a public facility and a free country, last I heard."

"No, you don't—"

She stood, aware she badly needed to leave the room.

"Excuse me, Special Agent—or whatever your title may be. You don't control me. I have a life—and things to do. Things that need to be done—here. Right here. Have a nice day."

She stood—with quiet dignity, she hoped— and headed quickly for the door.

How the hell could he still have such an effect upon her?

And why the hell did he have to be here now?

Another body. Another life cut tragically short. His job.

Brock was right; she was the one who shouldn't be here.

Chapter Three

To say that he'd handled his conversation with Maura badly would be a gross understatement.

But he couldn't start over. She was angry and not about to listen to him—certainly not now. Maybe later.

The library seemed oddly cold without her, empty of human life.

Brock needed to get going, but he found himself standing up, studying some of the posters and framed newspaper pages on the walls.

There was a rendering of the beautiful Gyselle, running through the woods, hair flowing, gown caught in a cascade.

Donald Glass didn't shirk off the truth or try to hide it; there were multiple newspaper articles and reports on the murders that had taken place in the 1970s.

And there was information on Francine Renault to be found, including a picture of her that was something of a memorial, commemorating her birth, acknowledging the tragedy of her death—and revealing that, while it was assumed she had been murdered by a disgruntled employee, the case remained unsolved.

Going through the library, Brock couldn't help but remember how shocked he had been to find himself under arrest. He'd been young— and nothing in his life had prepared him for the concept that he could be unjustly accused of a crime. He'd known where he wanted to go in life—but his very idealism had made it impossible for him to believe that such a thing as his being wrongly arrested could happen.

The world just wasn't as clean and cut-and-dried as he had once believed.

Of course, he had been quickly released— and that had been another lesson.

Truth was sometimes a fight.

And now, years later, he could understand Flannery's actions. There had been an urgency about the night; people had been tense. The police had been under terrible pressure.

Brock had usually controlled his temper— despite the fact that Francine had been very difficult to work with. But the day she had been killed, his anger had gotten the best of him. He hadn't gotten physical in the least—unless walking toward her and standing about five feet away with his fists clenched counted as physical. Perhaps that had appeared to be the suggestion of underlying malice. Many of his coworkers had known that he was always frustrated with Francine—she demanded so much and never accepted solid explanations as to why her way wouldn't work, or why something had to be as it was.

Like almost everyone else, he had considered Francine Renault to be a fire-breathing dragon. Quite simply, a total bitch.

She had been a thorn in all their sides. He had just happened to pick that day to explode.

After his blowup, he'd feared being fired—not arrested for murder.

He didn't tend to have problems with those he worked with or for—but he had disliked Francine. In retrospect, he felt bad about it. But she had enjoyed flaunting her authority and used it unfairly. Brock had complained about her to Fred Bentley many times, disgusted with the way she treated the summer help. Her own lack of punctuality—or when she simply didn't show up—was always for-given, of course, because she was above them all. That night, Brock had been quick to put Maura Antrim on the schedule—as if he had known that Francine wouldn't be there.

Until she was—dangling from the tree.

As the police might see it, after they'd been pointed straight at Brock by the mysterious anonymous tipster, he'd been certain to be on the tour when Francine's body had been dis-covered, a ready way to explain any type of physical evidence that might have been found at the History Tree or around it.

At the time, Brock had wanted nothing to do with Detective Flannery. He'd been hurt and bitter. He was sure that only his size had kept him from being beaten to a pulp during his night in the county jail, and once he'd been freed, he found that his friends had gone.

Including, he now thought dryly, the woman he had assumed to be the love of his life.

Maura had vanished. Gone back home, into the arms of her loving parents, the same people who had once claimed to care about Brock, to be impressed with his maturity, admiring of his determination to do a stint in the service first and then spend his time in college.

Calls, emails, texts, snail mail—all had gone unanswered. It hurt too much that Maura never replied, never reached out, and so he stopped trying. He had joined the navy, done his stint and gone on to college in New York.

And yet, oddly, through the years, he'd kept up with Michael Flannery. Now and then, Flannery would write him with a new theory on the case and apologize again for arresting Brock so quickly. Flannery wasn't satisfied; he needed an explanation he believed in. He explored all kinds of possibilities—from the familiar to the absurd.

Francine had been killed by an interstate killer, a trucker—a man caught crossing the Georgia state line with a teenage victim in his cab.

She had been killed by Donald Glass himself.

By college students out of Gainesville or Tallahassee, a group that had taken hazing to a new level.

She had even been killed, a beyond-frustrated Flannery had once written, by the devils or the evil that lived in the forest by the History Tree.

Frustration. Something that continued to

plague them. But then, Brock had been told that every cop, marshal and agent out there had a case that haunted them, that they couldn't solve—or had been considered closed, but the closure just didn't seem right, and it stuck in his or her gut.

Standing in the library wasn't helping any; Francine Renault had been a dead a long time, and regardless of her personality, she hadn't deserved her fate.

The truth still needed to be discovered.

More than ever now, as it was possible that her murderer had returned to kill again.

Brock left the library.

Before he left for his interviews in St. Augustine that day, he had to try one more time with Maura. He had to find her. He hadn't explained himself very well.

In fact, he had made matters worse.

He had known Maura so well at one time. And if anything, his faltering way of trying to get her far, far from this place, where someone was killing people had probably made her stubbornly more determined to stay.

He'd admit he was afraid.

Beautiful young women were disappearing,

and with or without his feelings, Maura was certainly an incredibly beautiful woman.

And there was more working against her.

She was familiar with the Frampton ranch and many of the players in this very strange game of life and death.

"MAYBE WE SHOULD move on," Maura said. She and Angie were sitting in the restaurant— Angie had actually wakened early enough for them to catch the tail end of the breakfast buffet, a spread that contained just about every imaginable morning delight.

The place was renowned for cheese grits; savoring a bite, Maura decided that they did remain among the best tasting she'd ever had. There were eggs cooked in many ways as well, plus pancakes, fruit, yogurt, nuts and grains and everything to cater to tastes from around the country.

Angie, too, it seemed, especially enjoyed the grits. Her eyes were closed as she took a forkful and then smiled.

"Delicious."

"Did you hear me?"

"What?"

"I was thinking we should move on."

Angie appeared to be completely shocked. "I… Yes, I mean, I know now about you—I mean, when you were a kid—but I thought we were fine. This is the perfect place to be home base for this trip. We can reach St. Augustine easily, areas on the coast—some of those amazing cemeteries up in Gainesville. I…"

She quit speaking. Nils Hartford, handsome in a pin-striped suit, was coming their way, smiling.

They were at a table for four and he glanced at them, brows arched and a hesitant smile on his face, silently asking if he could join them.

Angie leaped right to it.

"Nils! Hey, you're joining us?"

"Just for a minute. My people here are great—we have the best and nicest waitstaff, but I still like to oversee the change from breakfast to lunch," he said, sliding into the chair next to Maura. "You're enjoying yourself?" he asked Angie.

"I love it!" she said enthusiastically. "And last night—your brother was amazing. I mean, of course, I know that Maura had his job at one time, and I know Maura, and I know she was fantastic, but I just adored your brother. Keep him on!"

Nils laughed. "Oddly enough, that would have nothing to do with me. My brother reports directly to Fred Bentley, as do I. Couldn't get him hired or fired. But he's loved that kind of thing since we were kids. I was more into the cranking of the gears, the way things run and so forth." He turned toward Maura and asked anxiously, "And you—you okay being back here?"

"I'm fine," Maura said.

"Well, thank you both for what you're doing." He lowered his voice, even though there was no one near. "Even Donald is shaken up by the way we keep hearing that young women have been heading here or leaving here—and disappearing. Seriously, I mean, a tree can't make people do things, but… I guess people do see things as symbols, but—we're keeping a good eye on it these days. We never had arranged for any video surveillance because it's so far out in the woods—and nothing recent has had anything to do with the tree, but…anyway, we're going to get some security out there.

"Donald has a company coming out to make suggestions tomorrow. We have cameras now in the lobby, elevators, public areas…that kind of thing. But dealing with security and privacy laws—it's complicated. I mean, the tree is on Donald's property and it's perfectly legal to have cameras at the tree. And with today's tech—improving all the time, but way above what we had twelve years ago—the tree can easily be watched. Anyway, it's great that you're helping to keep us famous."

"A true pleasure," Angie told him.

He smiled at Angie and then turned back to Maura, appearing a little anxious again. "I just—well, I know you thought I was a jerk—and I was, back then. I did feel superior to the kids who had to work." He laughed softly and only a little bitterly. "Then the stock market crashed and I received a really good comeuppance. Odd, though. It's like 'hail, hail, the gang's all here.' Me, Mark, Donald, of course, Fred Bentley, other staff…and now you and Brock and Rachel."

"Rachel?" Maura echoed, surprised.

"Oh, you didn't know? Rachel is with the Florida Department of Law Enforcement now—she's working with Detective Mike Flannery. They've stationed themselves here—good central spot—for investigating this rash of disappearances. I think it's a rash. Well, everyone is worried because of the remains of the poor girl that were found at the laundry."

"Oh! Are you and Rachel still…a two-some?" she asked.

"No, no, no—friends, though. I have a lot of love for Rach, though I was a jerk to her when we were teens. I'm grateful to have her as a friend. And can you imagine—she's like a down and dirty cop. Not that cops can't be feminine. But she made a bit of a change. Well, I mean, she has nice nails still—she just keeps them clipped and short. Short hair, too. Good cut. She's still cute. But I hear she's hell on wheels, having taken all kinds of martial arts—and a crack shot. Great kid, still. Well, adult. We're all adults—I forget that some-times. And hey, what about you and Brock? I was jealous as hell of you guys back then, you know."

She certainly hadn't known.

"Of the two of us?" she asked. "And no—I hadn't seen him since that summer. I'm afraid that we aren't even social media friends."

"I'm sorry to hear that. But I guess that… Well, it was bad time, what happened back then." He brightened. "But you're here now. And that's great! I believe you recorded a tour?

And more, so far? I'd like to think that you could spend days here—"

"We *are* spending days here," Angie assured him. "I guess we're like the cops—or agents or officers or whatever. We're in a central location. We'll head to St. Augustine and come back here, maybe over Gainesville's way. It's just such a great location."

"Well, I'm glad. That's wonderful. If I can do anything for either of you..."

His voice trailed oddly. He was looking toward the restaurant entrance. Maura saw that Marie Glass had arrived and seemed to be looking for someone.

"Excuse me," he said, making a slight grimace. "Our queen has arrived. Oh, I don't mean that in a bad way," he added quickly. "Marie never meddles with the staff and she's always charming. I mean *queen* in the best way possible, always so engaging and cordial with the guests and all of us." He made a face. "She's even nice when she knows an employee is in trouble, never falters. Just as sweet as she can be—while still aloof and elegant. Regal, you know?"

"Yes, very regal," Maura agreed.

Marie was looking for Nils, Maura thought,

and as she noted their table and graced them with one of her smiles, Nils stood politely, awaiting whatever word she might have for him.

But she wasn't coming to speak with Nils. As she approached them, she headed for the one chair that wasn't occupied and asked politely, "May I join you? I'll just take a few seconds of your time, I promise."

"Of course, Mrs. Glass, please." Maura said.

Marie Glass sat delicately. "My dear Maura, you are hardly a child anymore, and though I do appreciate the respect, please, call me Marie."

Maura inclined her head. It was true. She was hardly a child. Marie simply had an interesting way of putting her thoughts.

"I know my husband and the staff here have tried to let you know how we appreciate the publicity your work here will bring us—and free publicity these days is certainly wonderful," Marie Glass began. "But we'd also be willing to compensate you if you want to show more of the resort—if you had time and if you didn't mind." She paused, flashing a smile Maura's way. "We love your reputations—and would love to make use of you in all possible ways. I am, of course, at your disposal, should you need help."

"Oh, that's a lovely idea," Angie said. "I'd have to switch up the format a little—as you know, I bring to light the unusual and frankly, the *creepy*, so—"

"Oh, bring on the creepy," Marie Glass said. She grinned again, broadly. "We do embrace the creepy, and honestly, so many people visit because of the History Tree. But we thought that allowing people to see how lovely the rest of the resort is... Well, it would make them think they should stay here and perhaps not just sign up for the campfire histories and the ghost walk into the forest. If it's a bit more comprehensive, we could use your videos on our website and in other promotional materials."

"I'm happy to get on it right away. Well, almost right away," Angie said cheerfully. "We did have plans to wander out a bit today, but we'll start on a script tonight. Maura's a genius at these things."

Maura glanced over at Angie, not about to show her surprise. So far, she hadn't known they were wandering out that day, and she wasn't sure that she was going to come up with anything "genius" after they got back.

From wherever it was that they were apparently going.

"Thank you ever so much," Marie said, standing. Her fingers rested lightly on the table as she turned to Maura. "We always knew our Maura was clever—we'd hoped to have her on through college and beyond, but, well...very sad circumstances do happen in life. Ladies, I will leave you to your day." She inclined her head to Nils. "Mr. Hartford, would you come to the office with me?"

As soon as they were out of earshot, Maura leaned forward. "Where is it that we're wandering off to today?"

"Well, it was your idea—originally, I'm certain," Angie said.

"Where?"

"St. Augustine, of course. You said it wasn't much of a drive and that we could easily get there and back in a day. I want to head to the Castillo de San Marcos—did you know that it's the oldest masonry fort in the continental United States? And I'm not sure how to say this, but St. Augustine is the oldest city in the country *continually* inhabited by European settlers. Think that's right. I mean, the Spanish started with missions and then stayed and… I have it all in my notes. Though I know you— you may know more than my notes!"

Maura glanced at her watch. It wasn't late— just about ten. If they left soon, they could certainly spend the afternoon in the old city, have dinner at one of the many great restaurants to be found—perhaps even hear a bit of music somewhere—and be back for the night.

"Okay," she said. "I had thought you wanted to finish up around here today—maybe even leave here and stay in St. Augustine or perhaps head out to the old Rivero-Marin Cemetery just north of Orlando. I just had no idea—"

"I thought you loved St. Augustine."

"I do."

"So it's fine."

"Sure. But we don't have permits, and while people film with their phones all the time now, what you're doing is for commercial purposes and—"

"We'll film out in front of places where I might need a permit to film inside. And if you don't mind, when we get to the square, I'll have you tell that tale about the condemned Spaniard who kept having the garrote break on him so that they finally let him go. Now, that's a great real story."

"The square is called the Plaza de la Constitución."

"Right. Yeah, but it's still a square," Angie said, grinning. "It is a square, right?"

"The shape is actually oblong."

"Okay, technicalities are important. But the story is great. About the man."

"His name was Andrew Ranson and he wasn't a Spaniard. He was a Brit and he had been working on an English ship and was accused of piracy. He absolutely declared that he was innocent but met his executioner with a rosary clutched in his hands. While he was being garroted, the rope broke, and the Catholic Church declared that his survival was a miracle. He recuperated, but when the governor asked that he be returned to be executed, the Church refused to give him back. He was eventually pardoned."

"And it's real—proving my desire to show all these stories. We're back to truth being far stranger than any fiction. And there's so much more. It is okay to go today, right?"

"Yes, it is, sure—let's sign this tab and get going right away."

Maura asked for the bill, but as she did so, her old boss came striding over to their table, a massive smile on his face.

Fred Bentley was powerfully built, stocky, not fat, but to Maura, it had always seemed that a barge was coming toward her when he strode in her direction.

He still had a head full of dark hair—dyed? She didn't know, but he had to be over fifty now, and it was certainly possible. He kept a good tan going on his skin, adding to his appearance of being fit, an outdoor man who loved the sun and activity.

He hadn't been a bad man to work for—he had certainly been better than Francine, who had changed her mind on a dime and blamed anyone else for any mistake.

Maura lowered her eyes for a moment, feeling guilty. Francine had not been nice. That didn't make what had happened to her any less horrible. Maura had to shake the image of Francine's lifeless body hanging from the tree. It haunted her almost daily.

"Maura, Angie," Fred said cheerfully. "Please, not a bill to be signed," he assured them. "What you're doing—in the midst of all this—is just wonderful. We're so grateful, honestly. Anything, anything at all that we can do, please just say so."

Maura smiled, uncomfortable. Angie answered him enthusiastically, telling him how she loved the grounds, the beauty of the pool and the elegance of the rooms, and, of course, most of all, the extra and unusual aspect of the campfire tales and the history walk. She was delighted to tout such a wonderful place.

To her surprise, Maura stood and listened and smiled, and yet, inside, she found that she was suddenly wondering about Fred.

Where was he when Francine Renault had been hanged from the great branches of the History Tree?

ST. AUGUSTINE WAS, in Brock's opinion, one of the state's true gems. Founded in 1565 by Pedro Menéndez de Avilés, the city offered wonders such as the fort, the old square, dozens of charming bed-and-breakfast inns, historic hotels, museums, the original Ripley's Believe It or Not! Museum, ghost tours, pub tours and all manner of musical entertainment.

The city also offered beautiful beaches.

But that day, he hadn't come to enjoy any of the many wonderful venues offered here.

As asked, Detective Rachel Lawrence had set up a meeting with Katie Simmons, the co-worker who had reported the disappearance of one of the missing women, Lydia Merkel. She was possibly the last one to see Lydia alive.

They were meeting at La Pointe, a new restaurant near the Castillo—Katie hadn't wanted to talk where she worked, though Brock intended to go by after their meeting, just to see if anyone else remembered anything that they might have missed when speaking with officers before.

The restaurant was casual, as were many that faced the old fort and the water beyond, with wooden tables, a spiral of paper towels right on the table and a menu geared to good but reasonable food for tourists.

Katie Simmons was there when he arrived; if he hadn't seen a picture of her in his files, he would have recognized her anyway. She was so nervous. She saw him as he entered through the rustic doorway, and her straw slipped from her mouth. She quickly brought her fingers to her lips as iced tea dribbled from them. She was a pretty young woman with soft brown hair and an athletic build, evident when she leaped to her feet, sat and stood once again.

She must have realized who he was by the way he had scanned the restaurant when he had entered. Maybe it was his suit—not all that common in Florida, even for many a business meeting.

She waited for him to come to the table.

He smiled, offering her his hand, hoping to put her at ease quickly.

"Katie, right?" he said.

"Special Agent McGovern?"

"Call me Brock, please," he said as he joined her at the table. "And please sit, and I hope you can relax. I can't tell you how grateful I am that you've agreed to speak with me. I know you've already told the police about Lydia, but as you know, we're hoping that we can find her."

Katie sat and plucked at the straw in her tea, still nervous. It looked as if tears were starting to form in her eyes.

"Time keeps going by… It's been weeks now. I don't know how she could still be alive."

A waiter in a flowered shirt was quickly at their table. Brock ordered coffee and he and Katie both requested the daily special, a seafood dish.

"I don't want to lie to you, but I also don't think you should give up," Brock told her when the waiter had gone. "People do just disappear—"

Katie broke in immediately. "Not Lydia! Oh, you had to know her. She was so excited to have moved here. She loved the city, loved working here—and there was more, of course. Lydia is a wonderful musician. She's magic with her guitar. She has the coolest voice—not like an angel, more like… I don't know, unique. She can be soft, she can belt it out… I love listening to her! She was going around getting gigs—and our boss is a great guy. He does schedules every week and talks to us before he sets them up. That allowed Lydia to set up her first few gigs."

"She was performing before she left here?" he asked.

"Oh, she only had two performances. One was for a private party out on a boat—but good money. They just wanted a solo acoustic player. And then another was at a place called Saint, which is a historic house that just became a restaurant—or kind of a nightclub. Can you be both? Or maybe you could say the same of a lot of places here—restaurant by day, club, kind of, by night with some kind of musical entertainment."

"Thanks. Do you know who hired her for the boat?"

"Sure. An association of local tourist businesses—it's called SAMM," she said and paused to grin. "St. Augustine Makes Money. That's really the name. Only you don't have to be in the city to belong—people belong from all kinds of nearby locations. In fact, half of the members, from what I understand, are really up in Jacksonville. We're the cute historic place, you know—Jacksonville is the big city. And where most people come in, as far as an airport goes." She grew somber again. "But she wasn't working the night before she disappeared. We were out together that night. She was leaving in the morning. She was so excited. Her career—her musical career—wasn't skyrocketing, but it was taking off."

"And according to what I've learned, she did leave in her own car."

"Yes, and she loved her car. It was old, but she kept it up—she kept great care of it. Oh, and that's why she chose her apartment. She could park there for free. Right in this area—well, out a bit—but still in what we consider the old section. I mean, you could walk to her place if you had to."

"Her car was never found," Brock noted. He'd read everything he could about Lydia before coming here today. And, of course, one of the reasons it was easy for law enforcement to consider the fact that she might have disappeared on purpose had to do with the fact that her car had never been found.

Katie was instantly indignant. "I know that—and I'm so sorry, but it made me wonder if the cops are stupid. The state is surrounded by water—oh, yeah, not to mention swamps and bogs and sinkholes and the damned frigging Everglades! Someone got rid of her car. I'm telling you—there is no way in hell that Lydia left here willingly—that she just drove away. Okay, I mean, she did drive away that morning, but... I didn't worry until I didn't hear from her. I know she would have called and texted me pics of the History Tree. When she didn't... I swear, I didn't panic right away, but when I didn't hear from her by that night, I knew something was wrong. I called the ranch, and they told me that she'd never checked in. That's when I called the police. And they all told me she might have just taken a detour. I told them that her phone was going straight to voice mail, and they still tried to placate me. I had to wait the appropriate time to even report her as a missing person with people really working on the case. Then I found out that two other young women had disappeared, and then…"

She broke off.

Brock continued for her, "And then they found the remains of Maureen Rodriguez. Katie, as I said, I don't want to give you false hope. But don't give up completely. People are working very hard on this now, I promise you." He hesitated—an agent should never make a promise he couldn't guarantee he could keep, but…

"Katie, I promise you, I won't stop until we know what happened to her."

She smiled with tears welling in her eyes.

"I believe you," she said.

Their lunches arrived. As they ate, Brock allowed her to go on about her friend. They hadn't known each other that long; they had just hit it off. She loved old music and Lydia loved old music. They had loved going to plays together, too, and were willing to travel a few hours for a show, and they both loved improv and ghost tours and so on...

He thanked her sincerely when the meal was over; she had taken his business card, but also put his direct line into her phone. He promised to call her when he knew something—good or bad—and they parted ways.

He decided to stop by the offices of SAMM next, wanting a list of those involved in the boat event during which Lydia Merkel had played, and then he'd be on to the restaurant where she'd entertained at her one gig on the mainland.

Someone, somewhere, had to know something.

Her car hadn't been found.

She'd only had one credit card; it hadn't been used outside the city. No one disappeared without a trace. There was always a trace.

He just had to find it.

Chapter Four

"I am standing here on Avenida Menendez in historic St. Augustine in front of a home that was originally built in 1763. While it was in 1512 that Juan Ponce de Léon first came ashore just north of here, and 1564 when French vessels were well received by the Native population, it was in 1565 that Pedro Menéndez came and settlement began.

"It was while the Spanish ruled in 1760—nearly two centuries later—that Yolanda Ferrer's father first built the house that stands behind me. In 1762, Spain ceded Florida to the British in exchange for Cuba, and Yolanda and her young husband, Antonio, left for Havana. But in 1783, Florida was ceded back to the Spanish in exchange for the Bahama Islands. Yolanda came back to claim the home her father had built, and the governor granted the home and property to her. At that time, she was a young and beautiful bride, and she thought that she and her husband would live happily ever after—but it wasn't to be.

"Yolanda, deceived by her husband, argued and pleaded with him not to leave her—and then either fell to her death or was, perhaps, pushed to her death, in the courtyard behind the house, where, today, diners arrive from all over the world to enjoy the fusion cooking of one of St. Augustine's premier chefs, Armand Morena.

"Through the years, the house has changed. It stood for a while as an icehouse and as a mortuary. For the last fifty years, however, it has changed hands only once, being a restaurant for those fifty years. But it wasn't just as a restaurant that the building was haunted by images of the beautiful, young Yolanda, sometimes weeping as she hurries along the halls, sometimes appearing in the courtyard and sometimes in what was once her bedroom and is now the manager's office. Yolanda is known to neither hurt nor frighten those who see her. Rather, witnesses to her apparition claim that they long to reach out and touch her and let her know that her story is known and that, even today, we are touched by her tragedy."

Maura finished her speech and waited for Angie to cut the take on the camera. Angie did so but awkwardly, and Maura thought briefly about the editing she was going to have to do. She much preferred it when Angie did the talking, but Angie had already spoken in front of the Castillo and Ripley's, and at the Huguenot Cemetery, the Old Jail, the Spanish Military Hospital Museum and several other places. She had begged Maura to let her do the filming on this one and Maura had acquiesced.

The sun was just about gone. And Maura was tired. As much as she loved St. Augustine, she was wearying of seeing it as if she was reliving that old vacation movie with Chevy Chase.

"Ready for dinner?" she asked Angie.

"Oh, you bet. We're going to have to come back. I loved what I called the square—the Plaza de la Constitución. I mean, that's the whole thing, isn't it? Executions took place there once, and now it's all beautiful, and there is a farmer's market, and people come for musical events and more. I love the streets surrounding it, the beautiful churches and all. I'm so glad we came."

"I've always loved this city," Maura agreed. "But I'm tired and starving. Have you picked out a place you'd like to go?"

There were plenty of choices.

Angie hesitated. She winced. "If I picked a particular restaurant, would you think that I was being ghoulish?"

Maura arched a brow warily. "Ghoulish? I don't know of any new horrific restaurant murders in St. Augustine."

"The restaurant is quite safe—no blood and guts in the kitchen or elsewhere, as far as I know," Angie assured her. "But…" she said and hesitated again. "It is the last place one of the missing girls had a music gig—I think I saw some video—because Lydia Merkel was playing her guitar and singing there not long before she disappeared. It's called Saint."

"Oh," Maura murmured. "Really, I'm not—"

"You wouldn't have even known, I don't think, if I hadn't told you."

Maura had read news reports; she had seen videos of the young women, including Lydia Merkel, who had worked here in St. Augustine, before her mysterious disappearance.

She hadn't remembered the name of the restaurant where the girl had played, nor even the name of the restaurant where she had worked.

"Please? I can't help but want to see it," Angie said.

Of course, Angie wanted to see it. If the poor woman's body was found and her murder was never solved, she would become another Florida legend.

She didn't have the energy to fight Angie, and besides, she doubted that the restaurant itself had been any cause of what had happened.

"Okay. Is it close? I'm sure you know. Are we walking? I don't think it existed the last time I was up here. I'll google it," she told Angie.

"Two blocks to the east and then one to the south," Angie said.

"We'll leave the car and walk."

Saint was like many restaurants in the historic district—once upon a time, it had been someone's grand home. Maura thought that it might have been built in the 1800s during the Victorian era; a plaque on the front assured her she was right: 1855. Originally the home of Delores and Captain Evan Siegfried.

Abandoned after the Civil War, it had become an institution for the mentally ill in the 1880s, a girls' school in 1910, a flower shop in the 1920s, a home again briefly in the 1950s before it was eventually abandoned—then recently restored by the owners of Saint.

The restaurant's original incarnation as a home was evident as they entered; there was a stairway to the second floor on the right, and on the left was what had once been a parlor— it now held a long bar and a few tables.

They were led around to what had probably been a family room; there, to the far rear, was a small stage, cordoned off now, but offering a sign that told them that Timmy Margulies, Mr. One-Man Band, would be arriving at 8:00 p.m.

As the hostess led them to their table, Maura stopped dead—causing a server behind her to crash into her with his tray and send a plate of gourmet french fries and something brown and wet and covered with gravy to go flying to the floor.

Maura was instantly apologetic, beyond humiliated, and—what was worse—she had stopped in surprise.

Brock McGovern was seated at a table near the door, deep in conversation with a woman who was wearing a polo shirt with the restaurant's logo but not the tunic worn by the waitstaff.

Of course, now he—like the rest of those in the place—was staring at her.

She truly wanted to crawl beneath the floor.

Apparently he admitted to the woman that he knew Maura; he was standing, about to head her way.

She winced and ignored him, trying to help the waiter whose tray she had upturned, stooping down to help.

"It's fine, it's fine—really!" the young waiter told her, smiling as he met her eyes, collecting fallen plates.

"Oh, dear," Angie murmured.

Then Brock was at her side with the woman who had been at his table.

"Miss, seriously, please, it's all right—this is a restaurant. We do have spills," the woman said.

"I know, but this one was my fault," Maura said.

She was startled when Brock took her arm. She looked up into his eyes and saw that she was overdoing her apology.

She was still looking at him, but she couldn't help herself.

"I am so, so sorry!" she said again.

"Maura, it's all right," he said quietly. And, looking back at him, she realized she was as attracted to the man he had become as she had been to the boy he had once been. And maybe, just maybe, she had been apologizing to him, and he had been telling her that it was all right.

But...

"You never tried to reach me," she blurted as the waiter and busboys—and whoever the woman with Brock was—all scrambled around, cleaning up.

His frown instantly assured her that something was wrong with that statement.

"I did try," he said. "Repeatedly. I called, and I wrote and... I guess it doesn't matter now. There's no way to change the past."

Angie cleared her throat, "Um, excuse me. I think that they want us to sit. Maybe get out of the way? Brock! Wow, weird coincidence. Nice to see you—want to join us? Maura, we really need to sit."

"Yes, of course," Maura said, wincing again—wishing more than ever that she could sink into the floor and disappear. Her mind was racing; she was stunned and felt as if she had been blindsided.

She had great parents. Loving parents. But had they decided that there was no proof that Brock had really been cleared—and that he shouldn't contact their precious daughter? What else would explain that he said he'd reached out but had never actually reached her?

She was still standing. And everyone was still looking at her.

She smiled weakly and took her chair, continuing to be somewhat stunned by Brock's words, wishing that they might not have been said under these circumstances. She supposed that was her fault. But she hadn't been able to stop herself.

"This is charming, absolutely charming," Angie said when they were seated, her eyes on Brock. "We had no idea that you'd be here—and even if we had, how convenient that we came to be in the same place! Have you had dinner? Will you join us for the meal?"

"I have not had dinner, though I did have a great lunch," he said.

"You were here investigating?" Angie asked.

"Yes."

"I know some of what's going on, of course," Angie said. "There's news everywhere these days—even on our phones. Hard to miss. I understand that the last girl who disappeared near the ranch had been living here in the city."

"Yes," Brock agreed. Angie frowned slightly; she'd obviously been expecting more info.

"Do you think there's any possibility of finding any of the missing women alive?" Maura asked him.

"There's always the possibility," Brock said.

"Ah," Angie said, studying him. "A politically correct answer."

"No," Brock said. "They haven't been found dead. That means there is a possibility that they will be found alive."

"Even after the woman's bones were found in sheets?" Angie asked.

"Even after that. It's still unknown if the cases are connected. That three young women have disappeared in a relatively short period of time does suggest serial kidnapping, but whether they were connected to the murder of Maureen Rodriguez is something that we still don't know. But," he added, "as I tried to say, I think it's a dangerous time right now for any woman from the ages of seventeen to thirty-five or perhaps on upward. Frankly, I'd be much happier if all those I knew were in Alaska right now—or Australia or New Zealand, perhaps."

He glanced over at Maura and she felt bizarrely as if her heart stopped beating for a minute.

She had been so angry for so long.

And now she realized that he hadn't been trying to get rid of her, per se—he was worried about everyone.

And maybe, because of the past, *especially* about her.

"But I do say it's a good thing that you stick together," he said, offering them a smile. "So, did you enjoy your day?" he asked politely.

Maura didn't have to worry about answering—Angie had no problem excitedly telling him about all that they had seen and done.

Their waiter—the same man who had collided with Maura—came and suggested that they have the snapper; the preparation of it, a combo of lemon and oil and garlic, was simple but exceptional. The three of them ordered. Maura and Brock were both driving, but Angie was at her leisure, so she indulged in the restaurant's signature drink—the Saint. It came out blue and bubbly, and she assured the waiter she didn't care much about what was in it. It was delicious.

"Have you all finished up here for the day?" Brock asked.

"Oh, yes, Maura is amazing. She knew where to go, what to get—we don't do full-length documentaries, you know. Just little bits. There have been all kinds of surveys about the modern attention span. You'll have tons of people look at something if it only takes them briefly out of their scanning. Unless it's something they really want to see, they pass right by when things become long. Two to three minutes tend to work really well for me. I was doing terribly, then I started working with Maura. She edits, although half the time we get just about perfect in one take."

He glanced over at Maura. "Are you in business together?" he asked.

"No," Maura said.

"Are you kidding? She's in megapopular demand!" Angie answered. "Artists, authors, performers—Maura knows how to make everyone really show off in that two to three minutes," Angie said.

"And I should definitely put in," Maura said quickly, "that Angie is truly a shooting star—

her books on truth being stranger than fiction, weird places and so on do amazingly well."

"I have some pretty generous sponsors for my video channel. Whoever knew that being a nerdy and somewhat gruesome kid would pay so well, huh?" Angie asked.

"We never do know where life will take us, I guess," Brock said, turning his attention to Maura once again. "But sometimes you pop before the camera?"

"When Angie wears out," Maura said.

"No, she's great," Angie said. "The video-cam thing loves her—and she's so smooth. A grand storyteller. She'd have been perfect in the old Viking days or in Ireland when history was kept orally and people listened around the fire. Of course, I keep telling her that it can't be her life. We've worked together about three years now and I'm always amazed that she never says no. Work, work, work, I tell her. I put things off when I'm in the middle of a relationship. Maura won't take the time for a relationship."

Maura glared at Angie, amazed that her friend would say such a thing—especially when she'd been flirting with Brock in front of Maura and was unabashedly interested in men. If not forever, for a night—as she had often said.

Maura wanted to kick her. Hard. Beneath the table.

And she might have, except that Angie was a little bit too far away to accomplish the task.

But Brock looked at Maura, something strange in his eyes. "Some of us do make work into everything," he said.

Angie pounced on that. "So—you're not married. Or engaged. Or steadily sleeping with anyone?"

Once again, Maura wanted to kick Angie. She damned the size of the table.

Brock laughed. "No, not married, engaged or sleeping with someone steadily. I think you only want to wake up every morning looking at someone's face on the other pillow when that person is so special that they know the good and the bad of you and everything in between. When you know... Well, anyway...my work takes up a lot of time. And it takes a special person to endure life with someone who works—the way I do." He sat back. "I'd like to follow you back to the Frampton ranch. Being perpetually, ever so slightly paranoid is a job hazard. I know you're fine, but...humor me?"

He was looking at Maura.

She still loved his face. His eyes, the contours of his cheeks, the set of his mouth. He'd been so determined and steady when they'd been young, and she had been so swept into... loving him. For good reason, she thought. He'd grown into the man she'd imagined somewhere in the back of her mind.

The man whose face she had wanted to see on the pillow next to hers when she woke up every morning.

"Maura?" Angie asked.

"Um, yes, sure," Maura said.

Brock stood, heading to find the waiter and pay the check.

"He is so hot!" Angie said. "He's got a thing for you. But if you're going to waste it—"

"Angie, he's working down here."

"You must have been the cutest kids."

"Oh, yeah, we were just frigging adorable, Angie. It was twelve years ago. Come on, let's get the car and head back. I have a lot of editing to do."

"No, you don't. Almost every take was perfect. I should have gotten that check—I'm really making money. Unless, of course, he has a budget for dinners out. I'd hate to ruin his budget."

"Angie, it's all right—look, he's motioning to us. We're all set to go."

Brock wasn't parked far away; he walked them to their car and then asked that they wait for him to come around on Avenida Menendez so that he could follow them.

As Maura waited behind the wheel, she thought about the years that had gone by.

She'd been stunned at first that things had ended so completely with Brock, but slowly, she'd felt that she was more normal—that heartbreak was a part of life. There had been other men in her life. But anytime it had gotten to *we're either going somewhere with this, or...*

She had chosen the "or."

She hadn't planned on making that choice forever, she'd just never met anyone else she wanted on the pillow next to hers every morning.

She wondered what it meant that he'd never found that person, either.

Brock drove up slightly behind her, allowing her to move into traffic. She headed out of the historic district of the city with him behind her, easily following.

"I wonder if I should have ridden with him," Angie said. She glanced over at Maura.

"I mean, if you're going to waste a perfectly good man…"

Maura was surprised that she could laugh. "Angie, I rather got the impression that you liked Nils Hartford or Mark Hartford. Maybe even Fred Bentley…"

"Bentley? No, no, no!" Angie said. "I like them tall and dark—or a little shorter but with that ability to smile and charm, something in their eyes, love of life, of who they are…not sure what. But Bentley? Nah. He's like a little tram coming at you—no, no. Although…" She turned in the passenger's seat to extend her seat belt, allowing her to look straight at Maura. "Now, I'd love to find out more about Donald Glass. Power and money! We all know that those are aphrodisiacs. Even when a man is sexually just about downright creepy. Somehow, enough money and power can change the tide, you know?"

"Uh, you know he's married," Maura reminded her.

"Ah, well, I heard that didn't always matter to him so much." Angie said. She laughed. "He even has a younger wife—younger than him. But that's the problem—there will always be younger, and younger will always be replaced with younger still."

"See, a warning philosophy," Maura said.

"But I know plenty of couples where there's an age difference—both ways!—who are happily going strong. I mean, there are older men who stay in love, and even older women who stay in love with younger men who stay in love."

"Of course," Maura murmured. She wasn't really paying attention to Angie anymore—she was only aware of the car following her.

It seemed forever before they reached the Frampton Ranch and Resort.

Angie talked the whole way.

It was all right. All Maura had to do was murmur an agreement now and then.

At long last, she pulled into the great drive and out to the guest parking. Brock was still right behind her, turning into a parking space just a few down.

He headed over to them while Maura went into the back seat of her car to grab her camera bag.

"An escort all the way," Angie said, greeting Brock as he joined them.

"All the way to the lobby," he agreed.

As they walked, Maura realized that despite the fact that he had joined them for dinner, she had never asked him about the woman in the Saint shirt who had been his companion at his table before she and Angie arrived.

But oddly, she didn't want to ask him in front of Angie. She glanced his way as they neared the entrance to the lobby, once the great entry to the antebellum house. He glanced back at her and, for a moment, it was strangely as if no time had passed at all. She'd always been able to tell him with just a look if they needed to talk alone.

He seemed to read her expression. Or, at least, she thought that he gave her a slight nod.

They walked up the porch steps and then through the great double doors to the "ranch house."

That was rather a misnomer. When the house had been built, it had been based on the Southern plantation style.

The integrity of the plan had been maintained with the registration desk to the far side and the doors leading to the coffee shop and the restaurant on opposite sides—one having once been the formal parlor and one the family parlor. The floors were hardwood, pol-

ished to a breathtaking shine without being too
slippery—a great accomplishment by maintenance and the cleaning crew. There were great
suites in the main house on the second floor
while the attic had been heightened and rooms
added there. Two wings—once bunkhouses—
had become smaller one-room rentals.

Angie had, naturally, taken one of the big
suites on the second floor.

Maura just hadn't needed that much space;
she'd been perfectly happy up in the attic, and
though she enjoyed working with Angie, she
liked her own room, her own downtime and
her own quiet at times.

"Safely in," Brock murmured.

"Welcome back...did you all decide to hit
the entertainments somewhere nearby together?" a voice asked.

Maura was surprised to see that Fred Bentley was behind the registration desk. There
was someone on duty twenty-four hours, but
it wasn't usually Bentley. He lived on the property, having something of an apartment at the
far end of the left wing, and she'd never really
figured out what he considered his hours to
be, but he was usually moving about in differ-

ent areas, overseeing tours, restaurants, house-keeping and everything else.

"Our night clerk didn't show," he said, apparently aware that they were all looking at him curiously. "Not appreciated," he added.

Maura didn't think that the night clerk would be on the payroll much longer.

"I ran into Maura and Angie in St. Augustine," Brock told him, answering Fred's earlier question. "It can be a surprisingly small world."

"That is a strange coincidence," Bentley said. "Well, as I said, welcome back. Oh, Angie, Mrs. Glass was hoping that you'd tour the place a bit with her tomorrow, get an idea of what you could do...more videos on the resort as a whole. The swimming pool and patio out back are really beautiful." He nodded toward Brock and Maura. "Those two used to love it—our summer employees have always been allowed use of the pool and gym during their off-hours."

"It was a great place to work," Brock said. "Well, it's been long day. I'm going to head up."

"I think we all are," Maura said. "Good night, Fred."

An elevator had been installed; Maura usually took the stairs, but Angie headed for them and she thought that maybe Brock was on the attic floor, as well. "Night, Angie," he said, heading for the elevator.

"Good night. But long day—I'll take the elevator, too!" she said, joining him and Maura, who pressed the call button.

"I'm in the Jackson Suite," Angie said. "Have you seen the suites?" she asked Brock cheerfully in the elevator. "You're welcome to come see my room."

"I've seen all the suites, and thank you, but tonight... I'm ready for bed," he told her.

Angie laughed softly and said, "Me, too."

Angie was always flirtatious—and she'd honestly stated what she wanted to Maura. Usually her easy way with come-ons didn't bother Maura in the least.

Tonight...

It wasn't the night. It was that she was coming on to Brock.

The elevator stopped on the second floor. Angie stepped out. "Well, lovely day, lovely dinner. Thank you both!"

"Thank you," Angie told her.

The elevator door closed.

"She's subtle, huh?" Brock murmured.

To her surprise, Maura smiled. "Very."

"So, what did you want to ask me?"

He could still read her glances. And in the small elevator, they were close. She wondered if it was possible for so much time to have gone by and there still be that something...

The elevator door opened. They stepped out into the hallway. Brock stood still, waiting for her to talk.

"None of my business really, but that was rather bizarre running into you. And you were with that woman at a table, and then just came on over with us so easily... I..."

"I went in search of Lydia Merkel," he said. "She had a coworker, Katie Simmons, who insists that Lydia didn't disappear on purpose. She'd gotten two gigs playing her guitar and singing, as well as working as a waitress. One of those gigs was at Saint."

"Oh! Well, yes, of course, you were working. And the woman you met... She hired Lydia Merkel?"

"Exactly. Lydia played there the Wednesday night of the week she disappeared. I was hoping to learn something more. But I pretty much gained the same information. The manager did have a few minutes to speak with Lydia. Katie said that she was the perfect entertainment for their night clientele—charming, speaking between songs, performing at just the right volume for diners. She asked her back for a few nights each week and Lydia was delighted. But she had a bit of a vacation planned. She was heading to the Frampton Ranch and Resort, and it was a long-held dream. The manager told her that was fine. Lydia could come in the next week and they'd discuss the future. Of course, as we all know, Lydia never went back."

He paused for a minute and said very softly, "I'm sorry. I never meant to come off the way that I did earlier. But a woman was murdered. Three young women are missing."

"I'm sorry, as well. I thought... Never mind. I don't know what I thought. But you seriously think that...there will be more kidnappings? And that the same person who murdered the poor woman whose remains were found at the laundry has taken these other women?"

He nodded grimly. "From what I've learned, there is no way Lydia Merkel just walked away from her life. I haven't had time for other interviews yet, but I imagine I will find that neither

Lily Sylvester nor Amy Bonham just walked away, either. And—while other businesses had sheets and used the laundry and fall in place with other leads as well, the Frampton Ranch and Resort still comes out on top of every list. Maybe I am touchy as far as this place goes, but in truth, I was sent here because of my familiarity with not just my home state but with the Frampton Ranch and Resort. You… you need to be so careful, Maura."

"I will be—I always am. But I'll be very careful. And…thank you."

He nodded. He knew that she was thanking him for the warning—and for telling her just how hard he had tried to reach her years ago.

He still hadn't moved; neither had she.

There were five rooms in the attic. The space was small. The walls were old and solid, and they were speaking softly, but it had grown late.

There was nothing more to say.

And there were years and years of words that they might say.

And, still, neither of them moved.

"I, uh… I'm so sorry for the families and friends of those poor women. And it's truly horrible about that young woman who was murdered, but do you think that they're all related?"

"We don't know. But they did have this place in common. And there's the past."

Maura shook her head. "You mean Francine?"

"Yes."

"But…that was twelve years ago."

"Yes."

"Peter committed suicide," Maura said. "I remember reading about it, and I remember him fighting with Francine. But then again, I remember everyone fighting with Francine. Still, with what Peter did…killing himself. Peter was a bit of a strange man with intense religious beliefs. He also had a temper, which usually came out as a lot of screaming and boiled down to angry muttering. It wasn't hard to believe that he had gone into a rage and dragged her out to the History Tree—and then been horrified by what he had done and regretted his action. Committed suicide."

"That's what was assumed. Never proved," Brock told her. "He was stabbed in the gut, something someone else could have done. Wipe the knife…put it in his hand. Leave him in the freezer. Easy to believe he might have done it himself. Especially when there were no other solid suspects. Just as easy to believe he was stabbed—and that the scene was staged."

He took a slight step back—almost as if he needed a little space. "Well, I'm in room three. I guess we should call it a night. I…uh… Well, you look great. And congratulations. I understand that you're doing brilliantly with your career. But I guess we all knew that you would. You're a natural storyteller—easy to see how that extends to directing people, to making them look great on video."

"Thanks. And you're exactly what you wanted to be—an FBI agent." She paused and took a deep breath. "And… Brock, I never received any of your messages. I don't know if my parents thought they were protecting me… They're good people, but… I am so sorry. I really had it in for you for years—I thought you just walked away."

He shook his head. Shrugged.

"Well, where are you?"

"I'm the last down the hallway, in five," she said.

"I'll watch you through your door," he said with a half smile. "I mean, I'm here—might as well see it through to perfect safety."

"Okay, okay, I'm going. I... I assume I'll see you," she murmured.

"You will," he assured her.

She turned and headed down the short hallway to the end. There, she dug out her key, opened her door, waved and went in.

Finally alone and in the sanctuary of her room, she leaned against the door, shaking.

How could time be erased so easily? How could the truth hurt so badly...and mean so very much at the same time? What would have happened if she had received his messages? Would they have been together all these years with, perhaps, a little one now, or two little ones...

She could have turned to him, laughed, slipped her arms around him. She knew what it would feel like, knew how he held her, cupped her nape when he kissed her, knew the feel of his lips...

Time had gone by. She hadn't received his messages.

She hadn't known he'd tried to reach her; she should have. As soon as she was home, her parents had gotten her a new phone with a new, unlisted number. They'd insisted that she change her email and delete all her social media accounts—not referencing Brock specifically, so much as the situation and the danger that could possibly still come from it.

Maybe she should have tried harder to get in touch with him. But when she'd never heard from him, she'd given up. Tried to move on.

Now they were living different lives.

She pushed away from the door. It had been a long day. She was hot and tired and suddenly living in a land of confusion. A shower was in order.

Maybe a cold shower.

She doffed her clothing, letting it lie where it fell, and headed into the bathroom. And it was while the water was pouring over her that she felt a strange prickle of unease.

It was like a perfect storm.

She was here. Brock was here…

Nils and Mark Hartford were here. Donald and Marie Glass… Fred Bentley…

And then, today her and Angie in St. Augustine, Brock in St. Augustine.

In the same restaurant. At the same time.

She turned off the water, dried quickly and stepped back out to the bedroom. She knew that Brock was working—that they all needed to be concerned. One poor woman was beyond help. Three were still missing, and maybe, just maybe...

There was nothing that she could do except, of course, be smart, as Brock had warned. And suddenly she couldn't help herself. She was thinking like Angie.

A night, just a night.

As Angie had made sure they all knew at dinner, Brock wasn't sleeping with anyone now in his life. There was no reason that the two of them shouldn't relive the past, if only for a night, for a few hours, for...

Memory's sake. If Maura just revisited the past, she might realize that it hadn't been so perfect, so very wonderful, that Brock wasn't the only man in the world who was so perfect...for her.

She knew his room number. It was wild, but...

Yes. It was too wild. She forced herself to don a long cotton nightgown and slip into bed.

And lay there, wide-awake, staring at the ceiling, remembering the contours of his body.

Chapter Five

Brock closed and locked his door, set his gun on the nightstand, and his phone and wallet on the desk by his computer. He shrugged out of his jacket and sat at the desk, opened his computer, keyed in his password and went to his notes.

He quickly filled in what he had learned that afternoon.

The most interesting had not been his conversation with the manager at Saint.

It had been earlier, when he had visited the offices of SAMM.

The event Lydia Merkel had played had been a social for members of the society. It hadn't been a mere boat, but the yacht *Majestic*, and fifty-seven members of SAMM had been invited.

Donald Glass and his wife had been among them.

The contact at SAMM had known that Maureen Rodriguez—or her sad remains at any rate—had been discovered. Every hotel, motel, inn and bed-and-breakfast that used the laundry facility had been questioned upon that finding. But no evidence had led to any one property.

Donald Glass knew about the women who had disappeared. He had never mentioned that he had met any of them.

To be fair, he might not have known that he had met Lydia Merkel. She had been working under her performance moniker—Lyrical Lee.

And, of course, the proprietors of many of the properties that used the laundry service were among those who had been on the yacht.

It was still a sea of confusion.

Except that Frampton Ranch and Resort was the location where the missing girls had been—or been headed to.

Brock filled in his notes, then stood, cast aside the remainder of his clothing and got into his shower. He needed to shake some of the day off. His puzzle pieces were still there, but he was missing something that was incredibly important.

Hard evidence.

And back to the old question—what the hell

could something that had happened twelve years ago have to do with the now?

And why, in the middle of trying to work all the angles of the crimes, concentrating on detail and logic, did he keep seeing Maura's face as she stood before him in the hallway?

He knew her so well. He smiled, thinking that she hadn't really changed at all.

She'd been polite, always caring, never wanting to hurt another person.

She'd been so stunned to see him in the restaurant and stopped short and then…

He smiled again, remembering her face. So mortified.

And then trying to clean up the mess herself because she'd caused it. When they had spoken…

She'd obviously been stricken, hearing that he had tried to reach her. He'd seen the pull of her emotions—she had to be angry with her parents, but they were good people and she did love them, and now, with the passage of time, she surely knew that they had thought they were doing what was best, as well.

He showered, thinking that washing away the day would help; sleep would be good, too, of course. He felt that learning about Lydia

Merkel and her aspirations to be a full-time musician were another piece of the puzzle—not because she entertained, but because of who she had done entertaining for: the hospitality industry—including the Frampton Ranch and Resort.

Brock and Maura had once been part of that. And they had intended to work part-time through college. His future had been planned out—he'd known what he was going to do with his life. And he had done it.

But Maura had always been part of his vision for his life, and maybe the most important part, the part where human emotion created beauty in good times and sustained a man through the bad.

He wasn't sure he ever made the conscious decision to go to her. He threw on a pair of jeans and left his room, years of training causing him to take his weapon and lock the door as he departed.

Which made him look rather ridiculous as he knocked softly on her door. When she opened it—he hoped and assumed she'd looked through the peephole before doing so—she stared at him wide-eyed for a minute, a slight smile teasing her lips—and a look of abject confusion covering her features.

"Um—you came to shoot me?"

She backed into the room. He entered, shaking his head, also smiling.

"Can't leave a gun behind," he told her.

"I see," she said.

For a moment, they stood awkwardly, just looking at each other, maybe searching for the right words. But words weren't necessary.

He set his holster and Glock down, fumbling blindly to find the dresser beside the door. He wasn't sure if she stepped into his arms or if he drew her in. But she was there. And time and distance did nothing except heighten each sensation, make the taste of her lips sweeter than ever. Their kiss deepened into something incredible. He felt her hand on his face, her fingers a gentle touch, a feathery brush, something unique and arousing, incredible and just a beginning.

His hands slid beneath the soft cotton of her gown and their lips broke long enough for him to rid her of it. He felt her fingers, teasing now along the waistband of his jeans. A thunderous beat of longing seemed to pound between them; it was his own heart, his pulse, instinctive human need and so much more.

Her fingers found the buttons on his jeans.

He couldn't remember ever before stepping from denim so quickly or easily.

Nor did he remember needing the feel of flesh against flesh ever quite so urgently.

They kissed again, his hands sliding down her spine, hers curving from his shoulders and down to his buttocks. They kissed and fell to the bed, and as his lips found her throat and collarbone, she whispered, "I was on my way to you."

He found her mouth again. Tenderness mixed with urgency, a longing to hold the moment, desire to press ever further.

It had been so long. And it was incredibly beautiful just to touch her again, hear her voice, bask in the scent of her...

Love her.

Familiar but new.

Their hands and lips traveled each other. He loved the feel of her skin, the curves of her body, loved touching her, feeling her arch and writhe to his touch.

Feeling what her touch did to him, hands traveling over his shoulders and his back; hot, wet kisses falling here and there upon him; that touch, ever more intimate.

As his was upon her. The taste and feel of her breasts and the sleekness of her abdomen, the length and sweet grace of her limbs.

And finally moving into her, moving together, feeling the rush of sweet intimacy and the raw eroticism of spiraling ever upward together, instinct and emotion bursting upon them with something akin to violence in their power, and yet so sweetly beautiful even then.

They lay together in silence, and once again he heard the beat, the pulse, his heart and hers, as they lay entwined, savoring the aftermath.

At last, he kissed her forehead, smoothing hair from her face.

She smiled up at him. "Twelve years," she said. And her eyes had both a soft and a teasing cast. "Worth waiting for, I'd judge."

"How kind. May I say the same?"

"Indeed, you may," she said, curling tighter against him. "You may say all kinds of things. Good things, of course. My hair is glorious— okay, so it's a sodden, tangled mass right now. My eyes are magnificent… Well, they are open. And, of course, you've waited all your life for me."

"I have," he said gravely.

She grinned at that. "You joined the FBI monastery?"

"I didn't say that. And I'm doubting you joined the Directors Guild nunnery."

She smiled, but she was serious, looking up at him. "I—I knew some good people."

"I would expect no less," he said softly.

"None as good as you," she whispered.

"Now, that can be taken many ways."

"But you know what I mean."

"I do. And don't go putting me on a pedestal. I wasn't so good—I was…a bit lost. The best way I had to battle it was to plunge head-on into all the plans I had made. Most of the plans I had made," he added softly.

"I am so sorry."

"Neither of us can be sorry," he assured her.

She kissed him again. For a while, their touching was soft and tender and slow.

But it had been so many years.

Somewhere in the wee hours, they slept. And when morning came, he awoke, and he saw her face on the pillow next to his. Saw her eyes open and saw her smile, and he pulled her to him, just grateful to wake with her by his side.

"Perfect storm," she murmured. "And I'm so sorry for the cause of it. So grateful for…you."

"We can't change what happened then. Now it's all right to be glad that we've…connected."

She nodded thoughtfully. "I keep thinking… there's something in history, something in the books, something that has to give us a clue as to what is going on."

"You need to stay out of it all," he told her firmly.

She rolled on an elbow and stared at him. "How? How would I ever really stay out of it? I was here when Francine was killed. That in itself…it's most horrible that a woman was so cruelly murdered, but, Brock…it changed everything. Changed us. And you do believe that what is happening now is related."

"There is really no solid evidence to suggest that," he said. "In fact, as far as profiling and evidence go, there is little reason to suppose that a killer might have hanged Francine—and then stuck around for over a decade to murder one young woman and kidnap three more. Really, the best thing would be for you to head to Alaska—as quickly as possible."

She smiled. "I would love to see Alaska one day. I haven't been. I'd love to see it—with you."

He was certain that, physically possible or not, his heart and soul trembled. They had just come together—tonight. And, well, thanks to Angie, they were both aware that nothing else had ever really worked for either of them in the years that had been lost between them.

He had never found *her* again. And she had never found him.

He grinned, afraid to let the extent of his emotion show.

"I don't think I have vacation coming anytime soon. But how about Iceland? What an incredible place for you to do legends and stories."

She was next to him, the length of her body close, and she touched his forehead, moving back a lock of his hair. "I don't work for myself—well, I do, but I'm a vendor hiring out my services. We need to be realistic. This is your work and more than your work. And now I'm working here, too. And I can help. I'm not stupid, Brock, you know that. I lock doors. I stay where there are other people. Whoever is doing this—be it a new thing or a crime associated with the past—they're smart enough to work in the shadows. No one is going to be hurt in the resort. You're in room three, and I'm in room five, and I'm not worried at all about the nights. Brock, I'm all grown-up. Quite a bit older than the last time, remember."

"And around the same age—"

"The missing women weren't wary or suspicious. They were just leading normal lives, trying to work and survive and simply enjoy their lives. Brock, most people are wonderful. They will lend others a helping hand. They just want the same things. Maureen Rodriguez was probably a lovely person—simply expecting others to be like that, too. From the little I know, the three missing women were probably similar—expecting human beings to act as human beings, having no idea that a very sick person was out there. I know that there's a predator. I won't be led astray, into any darkness—or off alone anywhere with anyone."

"Okay," he said quietly. "But if we're apart, I'll be calling you on the hour. Oh, screw the hour. Every five minutes, maybe."

"That will be fine. But unlikely. I think most of your interviews and investigations will take more than five minutes. And you really don't need to worry about me today—we'll be videoing out at the pool, in the restaurants—and I'm sure Angie would like to show herself speaking with Marie Glass—maybe Donald, too."

He heard a buzzing from the floor and leaped up. Luckily—he hadn't thought about it when he had left his room with just pants and his Glock—his cell phone was in the pocket of his jeans.

He dug for his phone.

"Yeah, Mike," he answered, having seen the detective's name on his caller ID.

"I'd like you to come with me to the Gainesville County morgue," Flannery said.

Brock gritted his teeth; the morgue meant a body. A body meant that his actions thus far had failed to save anyone.

"One of the missing girls?"

"I don't think so—I believe—or the ME there has suggested—that the remains are much older. But… Well, I'll fill you in. How soon can you be ready?"

"Ten minutes," Brock said.

"Better than me. Meet you downstairs in fifteen. We can grab coffee and head out."

"I'll be there."

"First man to arrive orders the coffee. Never mind—Rachel will beat us both. She'll order it."

"I'll be down."

He hung up and slipped into his jeans, looking back at the bed. Maura was up, staring at him, her face knit into a worried frown.

"I have to go... Not sure when I'll be back. Keep in touch, please. And stick with Angie and Marie Glass—and don't go walking into any old spooky woods, huh, okay?" he asked.

She smiled. "I promise," she told him. "But—"

"Old bones—we have to see what they are. And no—not one of our three missing girls. You'll be here all day?"

She smiled back at him.

"I'll be here all day," she assured him.

He hurried out of her room, heading to his own, hoping he wouldn't run into anyone while he was clad in his jeans only—but not really caring.

He would shower, dress and be ready in ten minutes. He wasn't worried about that.

He did hate that he was leaving.

And hoped it was something he was going to have to get used to doing.

MAURA WAS HAPPY—and determined. No, she wasn't an agent. Or a cop of any kind. No—

she wasn't even particularly equipped to defend herself should she need to do so.

But she was smart and wary and everything else that she had told Brock.

Like it or not, she had been at the ranch when Francine was killed. And she was here now, and she was a Floridian and these horrible things were happening in her state. Today she would be filming around the estate with Angie and Marie, and she'd be speaking with all those here as much as possible—especially Fred, Marie, maybe Donald and Nils and Mark.

Her reasoning might be way off. Just because they had all been here twelve years ago and were here now didn't mean a thing. The solution to Francine's murder and answers about the girls who were dead and missing now might be elusive. It was sad but true that an alarming percentage of murders went unsolved. She'd read the statistics one time— nearly 40 percent of all homicides in the US went unsolved each year.

Except on this, while it was in his power, she knew that Brock wouldn't let go.

So, in her small way, she would do her best. And maybe that meant going through the library again—finding out everything she could about the Frampton Ranch and Resort—and the people who were here.

Maura showered, dressed and set out to edit some of her video from the day before. At nine she decided to go down to breakfast; Angie, she knew, would wake up when she was ready and come down seeking coffee.

Maura took her computer with her, curious to see what various search engines brought up on the ranch. As with most commercial properties, the results showed every travel site on the planet first. And the history of North Central Florida didn't provide any better results. She didn't find much that was particularly helpful—nothing she didn't know already.

Frustrated, she was about to click over into her email when she noticed a site with the less-than-austere title of Extremely Weird Shit That Might Have Happened.

Once there, she read about a strange organization that had sprung up in the area in the 1930s. Various local boarding schools and colleges had provided the members—usually rich young men with a proclivity for hedonistic lifestyles. They had created a secret society known as the Sons of Supreme Being, and considered themselves above others, apparently siding with the Nazi cause during World War II, dissolving after the war, but supposedly surfacing now and then in the decades that followed.

They had been suspected of the disappearance of a young woman in the 1950s, but it had been as difficult for police to prove their complicity as it had been to prove their existence. Members were sworn to secrecy unto death, and in the one case when a young man had admitted to the existence of the society and the possible guilt of the society in the disappearance of the girl, that young man had been found floating in the Saint Johns River.

"My dear Maura, but you are involved in your work!"

Startled, Maura looked up. Marie Glass had come to her table. She was standing slightly behind her.

Maura quickly closed her computer, wondering if Marie had seen what she'd been reading.

"I'm so sorry," she said. "Have you been waiting on me long?"

"No, dear, I just saw the fascination with which you were reading!" Marie said, sliding into the seat across from her. "Today is still a go, right? You and Angie will shoot some of the finer aspects of the resort?"

"Oh, yes, we're all set," Maura said. "Or we will be, once Angie is down."

"That's lovely. I thought we'd start with the pool and patio area, maybe scan the gym so that people can see just how much the resort offers? I know that Angie's forte lies in a different sort of content—as does yours—but she does have such an appeal online. She reaches a big audience. I can't help but think it'd be good exposure."

"Of course. Whatever you'd like."

"It's lovely that Angie Parsons will use her video channel for us."

"She couldn't wait to come here. She's fascinated with the resort."

"Well, her fascination was with the History Tree—" She paused a bit abruptly, then smiled. "I've seen some of Angie's videos and heard her podcasts and I even saw her speak at a bookstore once. The tree does seem right up her alley. And, of course, since it does seem to draw much of our clientele, I do appreciate the tree. Or trees. But… Well, those of us who knew Francine can't help but take that all with a grain of salt. Anyway…when do you think we'll be able to get started?"

"I imagine Angie will be down anytime," Maura told her. "I don't want to see you held up, though. Do you want me to call you when she's had her coffee?"

"Well, dear, this is my plan for the day, but if you could… Oh, there she is now," Marie said with pleasure.

Maura turned toward the entry to the coffee shop. Angie was walking in with Nils Hartford. She was her smiling, bubbling, charming self, talking excitedly.

She saw Maura sitting with Marie and waved, excused herself to Nils and came over. "Good morning. Mrs. Glass, you are bright and early."

Marie slowly arched a silver brow. "If one can call ten in the morning early, Angie, yes, I am bright and early." Apparently in case her words had been too sharp, she added, "But I'm certainly grateful for your work and ready whenever you are."

"Right after one coffee," Angie said. "One giant coffee!"

"Wonderful. I'll just check on the patio area

and make sure someone's darling little rug rat hasn't made a mess of the place."

Marie rose and smiled again, perhaps trying to take the sting from her comment. "At your leisure," she said and sailed out of the coffee shop.

Angie made a face and sat. "If America had royalty, she'd be among it. If she hadn't been born into it, she would have married into it. Oy!"

"She is a bit..."

"Snooty?" Angie said.

Maura shrugged.

"Kind of strange, don't you think?"

"What's that?"

"Donald doesn't seem to be as...well, snooty. Best word I can come up with."

"To be honest, I don't know either of them that well. I mean, I worked for them before, but I was among the young staff—they hardly bothered with us. Fred was our main supervisor at the time."

"Along with Francine Renault?" Angie asked.

"Yep."

"And wasn't your beau kind of like the ranking student employee here?"

"Yes."

Angie smiled and leaned toward her. "And?"

"And what?"

"What about last night?"

"What about it?"

"Oh, you are no fun. Details. Ouch! You can feel the air when you two are close together. I'll admit—well, I don't need to admit anything, I frankly told you that I was deeply into him."

"Angie, you're deeply into a lot of people."

"True. So I've turned my attention to Nils. He is a cutie, too. Maybe even more classically handsome. Not as ruggedly cool—not like fierce, grim law enforcement. But damned cute. And, hmm, we are here a few more days. I do intend to have some fun."

"Angie—"

"Yes, I mean get laid!" Angie laughed at Maura's reaction. "Too graphic and frank for you? Oh, come on, Maura, you know me."

"And I wish you luck in your pursuits. I'm sure you'll do fine."

"Ah, you see, I shall do as I choose, which is much better than fine." Angie frowned suddenly. "Where is your law-and-order man?"

"He's here working, Angie. He went off—to work."

"Well, I suppose we should work, too. Let me grab my coffee."

"Great. I'll run my computer up and grab the camera."

Angie didn't need to get up for her coffee; Nils arrived at their table with a large paper cup.

"Two sugars, a dash of cream, American coffee with a shot of espresso," he said, delivering the cup to Angie. Her fingers lingered over his as she accepted the drink.

"Thank you so much," Angie said, smiling at him brilliantly. "When we talk about the restaurants, you will be in the video with me, won't you?"

"My absolute pleasure," Nils assured her. He smiled over at Maura. "Morning. I saw you earlier, but you were so involved, I didn't want to interrupt."

"You can interrupt anytime," Maura told him. "I was really just web browsing."

"Anything in the news—or have Brock or that Detective Flannery made any progress on

the missing girls? Or, wow, I keep forgetting—
Rachel?"

"Not that I know about."

"Something is going on this morning. There
was a discovery just south of the Devil's Millhopper," Nils said. "I saw it on the news.
Human remains were found. A Scout troop
discovered them during a campout."

"I—I probably should have started with the
news," Maura said. "I didn't." She didn't tell
him that she knew something had been found
because Brock had taken off early with Detectives Flannery and Lawrence to investigate.
"More human remains. How sad."

Angie didn't seem concerned. "The Devil's Millhopper?" she asked. "That's…a cool
name. What the hell is it?"

"A sinkhole," Maura told her. "Devil's Millhopper Geological State Park—it's in Gainesville. It's a really beautiful place, a limestone
sinkhole about 120 feet deep. The park has
steps all the way down, a boardwalk—sometimes torn up by storms—and beautiful nature
plants and trees and all that."

"We need to go there," Angie said. "How
did I miss a sinkhole?"

"I don't think it's haunted. But, hey, who

knows? Anything can be haunted, right?" Nils asked. "It's not all that far from here—a cool place. Hey, I'd love to take you. I have a day off coming up, if you want to go."

"I'd love it if you could go with me... We'll need Maura, of course, for the video," Angie said.

"I'd love to go with both of you," Nils said.

While Angie smiled back at him, Maura found herself remembering the Nils she had known before—the young man who had thrived on being so superior. She tried to remember if she had noted any of his interactions with Francine. Francine most probably wouldn't have reacted to any of his behavior.

Could Francine have angered Nils...and could he, at eighteen, have been capable of murder?

Ridiculous. He'd been the same age as Brock; they'd all just been kids.

"Seriously, I love the park, too," Nils said, looking at Angie and then flashing a quick smile at Maura. "It's really a pretty place."

"Isn't Florida at sea level? Doesn't it flood?" Angie asked.

Nils looked at Maura again and shrugged. For a moment, he just looked like a nice—and attractive—man. One with a sense of humility—something he had once been lacking.

"Hey, we even have hill country in this area. But honestly, I don't know. It's a sinkhole. It has something to do with the earth's limestone crust or whatever. Geology was never my forte. Hey, we really do have hills in the state—not just giant Mount Trashmores, as we call them. And we have incredible caverns and all kinds of things. Most tourists just want warm water and the beaches, but it's a peninsula with all kinds of cool stuff. I'll find a ghost there for you if you want!"

Angie laughed and even Maura smiled.

"Great—we'll set it up," Angie said.

Maura quickly stood. "Meet you by the pool," she told Angie.

She clutched her computer and ran up both flights of stairs to her room. Housekeeping had already been into her room, she saw.

It seemed so pristine now. Cold.

Maybe just because Brock was no longer there.

She shook her head, impatient with herself. And for a moment, she paused. Being with him again had been so easy, so wonderful, so... perfect.

And she was, perhaps, wrong to dwell so much on one night. Things had torn them apart before.

She was suddenly afraid that events might just tear them apart again.

"WHEN REMAINS ARE down to what we have here," Dr. Rita Morgan told them, "it's almost impossible to pinpoint death to months, much less days and weeks. The bones were found just south of the Devil's Millhopper, as you know, deep in a pine forest. The area was just outside a clearing where the Scouts set up often, but not in the clearing, and it was only because a boy went out in the middle of the night to avail himself of a tree—no facilities out there, camping is rugged—that he came across them. Of course, the kid screamed and went running back for his leader or one of the dads along on the trip, and the dad called the police and… Well, here we are. The bones were scattered and we're still missing a few. I believe that all kinds of creatures have been gnawing upon them, but…there are marks— here, there—" she pointed to her findings "—that were not made by teeth. This young woman—we did find the pelvis, so we can say she was female—was stabbed to death. Oh, these are rib bones I'm showing you with the knife marks. I guess you figured that."

Brock nodded, as did Michael Flannery and Rachel Lawrence.

They were all familiar with the human skeletal system.

"But you think that she was killed sometime in the last year?" Brock asked.

"The integrity of the bone suggests a year— and a few teeth were left in the skull," Dr. Morgan explained. "I'm going to say that she was killed sometime between six and twelve months ago. She was most probably buried in a very shallow grave in an area where the constant moisture and soil composition would have caused very quick decay of the soft tissue, and insects and the wildlife would have finished off the rest. We're still missing a femur and a few small bones. And I'm afraid so many teeth are missing I doubt we'll ever be able to make an identification. We can pull DNA from the bones and compare to missing persons, but as you know, that will take some time."

"She's not one of the three recently missing women, though, right? We are talking at least six months?" Brock asked.

"At least six months," Dr. Morgan agreed. She indicated the pile of bones that were all that was left of a young life, shaking her head sadly. "I wish I could tell you more. She was somewhere between the ages of eighteen and thirty, I'd say. Again—the pelvis is intact enough to know that. We'll keep trying—we'll do everything that we can forensically."

They thanked the doctor and left the morgue.

Outside, Michael Flannery spoke up. "I think that whoever killed Francine Renault twelve years ago got a taste for murder—and liked it. I think that whoever it is has been killing all these years. Maybe slowly at first, fewer victims. I'm not a profiler, but I've taken plenty of classes with the FBI—and I'm sure that you have, too. He's speeding up—for years, he was fine killing once a year. Now—or in the last year—he's felt the need becoming greater and greater."

"It is a possibility," Brock said. "Michael, it is possible, too, that whoever killed Francine did so because she was really unlikable and made someone crack—and that these two dead women we've found have nothing to do with Francine's death. And that the kidnappings aren't associated, either."

Rachel shook her head. "You're playing devil's advocate, Brock."

He was. Brock didn't know why—maybe just too much pointed to the Frampton Ranch and Resort, and he didn't really want it to be involved. Despite what had happened, he had a lot of good memories from his time there.

They now had the bones of two women killed within the past year. Three women were still missing. He'd barely had a chance to scratch the surface of what was going on.

"Come on, Brock. I've been chasing this for twelve years," Flannery said. "I did something I came to learn the hard way simply wasn't right—and now I'm chasing the results of my mistake."

"It wasn't your mistake. You weren't high enough on the food chain back then to insist that the case not just remain open, but that it continue to be investigated with intensity," Brock said. "But say your theory is right. If the killer is at large, then the killer hanged Francine and stabbed Peter Moore to death to make it appear like a suicide and provide a fall guy. That may have been where the killer decided stabbing afforded a greater satisfaction than watching someone strangle to death."

"Where they got a taste for blood," Flannery agreed.

"And you think it's someone who was or is still involved with the Frampton ranch," Brock said.

Rachel watched them both. "Honestly, Nils Hartford was a bona fide jerk—but I don't believe he was a killer," she said, though neither of them had accused Nils. "He… I mean, he and I were never going to make it, but we did become friends. When his family lost all their money, he admitted to me that he loved restaurants and he loved the ranch and that he believed Fred might give him a chance. And as to Mark… Mark was just a kid."

"Kids have been known to be lethal," Flannery reminded her.

"Fred Bentley?" Brock asked, looking at Rachel. "He wasn't a bad guy to work for—and I think he was well liked by the guests. He's still holding on to his position."

"And he'd oversee any laundry sent out by the hotel," Rachel said.

"If not Bentley…and you're right about the Hartford boys…"

"That leaves Donald Glass himself," Brock said.

Donald Glass—who was married. Who, it

had been rumored, had been indulging in an affair with Francine Renault.

A man who had acquired quite a reputation for womanizing through the years.

But would a man brilliant enough to have doubled a significant family fortune have been foolish enough to commit murder on his own property—and leave clues that could lead back to him?

"Time to head back," Brock said. "I say we casually interview all of our suspects. Let them in a little on our fear that the three missing women are dead—and that there is, indeed, a serial killer on the loose."

"Can you get someone at your headquarters tracing the movements of our key possible suspects at the ranch?" Flannery asked Brock. "FDLE is good—but your people have the nation covered."

"Of course," Brock said. He hesitated. "I haven't spoken with Glass that much, but he expressed pleasure that we chose his place as a base. Of course, it's possible that such a man thinks of himself as invincible. Above the rest. But still, I'd say there's another major question that needs to be answered."

"What's that?" Flannery asked.

"Where are the missing women? There are no bodies. Of course, it's difficult for police when adults disappear—they have the right to do so, and often they have just gone off. But the woods were searched. Bodies weren't found. If it's Glass committing these crimes—or someone else at the Frampton property or someone not involved there at all—he might be taking the women somewhere. Keeping them—until he kills them. If we can find that place…maybe we can still save a few lives."

"And maybe we're all barking up the wrong tree," Rachel said. "And if we concentrate too hard in the wrong direction…well, there go our careers."

"We have to put that thought on hold—big thing now is to find the truth and hope that we can find the missing women. Alive," Brock said. "Agreed?"

Rachel winced. "Right, right. Agreed."

"Agreed. Oh, hell, yeah, agreed," Flannery said.

Brock didn't like what he was coming to believe more and more as a certainty.

A killer was thriving at the Frampton Ranch and Resort.

And Maura was there.

A beautiful young woman who had a history with the ranch.

A perfect possible victim.

Ripe for the taking.

Except that he wouldn't allow it. God help him, he'd never allow it.

He had found her again; he would die before he lost her this time.

Chapter Six

Maura and Angie wrapped up at the pool. Out in the back of the main house and nestled by the two wing additions, the pool was surrounded by a redbrick patio. While the many umbrellas and lounge chairs placed about the pool were modern and offered comfort and convenience, the brick that had been set artfully around managed somehow to add a historic touch that made it an exceptional area.

Maura didn't have to appear on camera; she took several videos of the pool itself and then several with Angie and Marie Glass seated together, sipping cold cocktails, with Marie talking about the installation of the pool twenty years earlier and how carefully they had thought about the comfort of their guests.

A young couple had come out while Maura was filming the water with the palms and other foliage in the background. They'd been happy to sign waivers and be part of the video—laughing as they splashed each other in the water.

When Maura's cell rang, she was so absorbed in detail that she almost ignored it—then she remembered that she and Brock had made a pact and quickly excused herself to answer the phone, leaving Angie and Marie to sit together chatting—just enjoying the loveliness of the pool and one another's company. It was evident that Marie did admire Angie very much. The two women almost looked like a pair of sisters or cousins sitting there, chatting away about the adults around them.

Maura turned her back and gave her attention to the call.

Brock sounded tense—he reminded her to stay with Angie and in a group at all times.

"I won't be leaving here," she assured him. "I'm with Angie and Marie. We're going to go film the restaurants and then the library. We'll probably record in Angie's suite. Are you heading back?"

He was, he told her.

She smiled and set her phone down and

looked at Angie and Marie, who were watching her, waiting politely for her to finish her call.

"Onward—to the restaurant," she said.

"Perfect. They won't open for lunch for another twenty minutes," Marie said. "We can show all the tables and will let Nils describe some of our special culinary achievements."

"Yes. Perfect," Maura said.

"Oh, yes, that will be wonderful—we'll have the daily specials, and Nils can serve them. First, Maura can take the restaurant empty, and then some of the food—it's going to be great!" Angie said, always enthusiastic.

Angie and Marie went ahead of Maura; she collected her bag and the camera and expressed her appreciation to the young couple again.

They thanked her—they couldn't wait to send their friends to Angie's web channel when the video was posted.

Maura hurried after Marie and Angie.

The restaurant was pristine when they went in—set for lunch with shimmering water glasses and wineglasses and snowy white tablecloths. The old mantel and fireplace and the large paned windows created a charming atmosphere along with all that glitter. Angie did a voice-over while she scanned the restaurant.

Nils stood just behind Maura; that made her uneasy, but she wasn't alone in the restaurant, she was with Marie and Angie, and a dozen cooks and waitstaff lingered just in the kitchen. She knew that she was fine.

She wondered if Nils made her nervous because she did suspect him of something, or...

If she was just nervous because she didn't like anyone at her back.

When Nils touched her on the shoulder, she almost jumped. "Sorry, sorry!" he said quickly. "I don't want to mess this up—if I do something wrong, you'll tell me, right? You'll give me a chance to do it over?"

"Nils, this is digital. We can do things as many times as you want, but I believe what we're trying for is very spontaneous, natural— just an easy appreciation for what the resort offers."

"Okay, okay—thank you, Maura," he said.

She smiled. "Sure."

Marie was going to sit with Angie. Before she could, there was a tap on the still-locked door. "Let me just tell them we'll open in a few minutes, right at twelve," Nils said.

Angie and Marie took a seat at a circular table for two right by a side window.

But Nils didn't come back alone.

Donald Glass, elegantly dressed in one of his typical suits and tall and dignified—as always—arrived with him.

"I'd thought it would be good if I popped into one of these videos Marie thinks will be such a thing. If you don't mind. Darling," he told Marie, "would you mind? I think I speak about our wine list with the most enthusiasm."

"No, darling, of course, you must sit in," Marie said.

She rose, giving up her seat. "I'd have thought you might want to do the library," she said. "You do love the library so."

He grinned. "Yes, I'm proud of my libraries. But even then…good wine is a passion."

"Okay, dear."

Maura thought that Marie seemed hurt, but she really didn't show anything at all. She smiled graciously, telling Nils, "They'll need the menus and wine lists."

"Already there, Mrs. Glass, already there," Nils said.

"Okay, then," Maura said. "In five, four…" She finished the count silently with her fingers.

"Angie Parsons here, and I'm still at the Frampton Ranch and Resort. After a day at the oh-so-beautiful pool—and before a night at the incredible historic walk—there's nothing like a truly world-class dinner. And I'm thrilled to be here with Donald Glass, owner of this property and many more, and—perhaps naturally—a magnificent wine connoisseur, as well."

"Thank you so much, Angie. Marie and I are delighted to have you here. I do love wine, and while we have Mr. Fred Bentley, one of finest hotel managers in the state, and Nils Hartford, an extraordinary restaurateur, manning the helm, no wine is purchased or served without my approval." He went on to produce the list, explaining his choices—and certainly saying more in a few words than Maura would ever know, or even understand, about wine.

But the video was perfect on the first take.

Nils came in as they discussed the menu. He spoke about the excellence of their broad range of menu choices. He suggested that Angie enjoy one of their fresh mahi-mahi preparations, and that Donald order the beef Wellington. That way they could indulge in bites of each other's food.

He might have been nervous, but he did perfectly.

"And now we really have to open the restaurant," he said.

Donald Glass smiled and nodded. "No special stops—we run a tight ship. But, of course, that will be fine, right, Maura?"

"That will be fine. I can avoid other tables, not to worry," she said.

But people were excited when they noted that something was going on.

Many had been at the campfire when she had filmed.

They wanted to be involved.

As she spoke to other diners pouring in, Maura knew that Marie Glass was watching her. She turned to her.

"Is that okay?" she asked.

"Yes, yes, lovely," Marie said. She glanced back at Donald, chatting away still with Angie at the table.

They were laughing together. Angie was her

ever-charming self—flirtatious. She basically couldn't help it. Glass was enamored of her.

Marie looked back at Maura, her eyes impassive. "Indeed, please, if others wish to sign your waivers, it will certainly add on. Hopefully the food will come out quickly for my husband and Miss Parsons, and we'll be moving on. I can lock down the library, though, of course, Donald will want to be on the video then, too, as I suggested earlier."

"Thank you," Maura told her.

Marie was at her side as she chose a table close by to chat with the guests and diners who arrived—wanting to be on video.

She was startled when she accepted the last waiver and Marie spoke.

But not to her…

Not per se.

She spoke out loud, but it was as if she believed that her words were in her mind.

"And I have always vouched for him. Always," she murmured.

"Pardon?" Maura said.

"What? Oh, I'm so sorry, dear. I must be thinking out loud."

She walked away; Maura went to work.

The head chef himself, a new man, but well

respected and winner of a cable cook-off show, came out to explain his fusions of herbs and spices with fresh ingredients.

The videos were coming out exceptionally well, Maura thought.

But she couldn't help remembering the way Donald Glass had sat with Angie—and the way Marie reacted to her husband.

BROCK WAS PARKING the car when he received a message from his headquarters. He hadn't contacted Egan. He had gotten in touch with their technical assistance unit and had reported on the remains that had been found, but it was Egan who called.

Egan wanted to know about the body that they had seen that morning; Brock told him their working theory, thinking that Egan might warn them against it.

He didn't.

Then he put Marty Kim, the support analyst who had been doing extra research for Brock's case, on the phone.

"I did some deep dives this morning," Marty told him. "Before coming to the Frampton Ranch and Resort, Nils Hartford was working at a restaurant in Jacksonville, Hatter and Rabbit. Trendy place. He left there for the Frampton resort, but there was a gap between jobs. I found one of the managers willing to talk. Nils resigned—but if he hadn't, he would have been fired. There was a coworker who complained about sexual harassment. Hartford was managing. The young woman was a waitress. She told the owner that she was afraid of Nils Hartford."

"Interesting. And do we know if the waitress is still alive and well?"

"Checking that out now," Marty told him. "I can't find anything much on Mark Hartford. He went to a state university, majored in history and social sciences, came out and went straight to work for Donald Glass."

"Fred Bentley?"

"He's been with Glass for nearly twenty years—at the Frampton Ranch and Resort for fifteen of them. Before that, he was working at a big spread that Glass has in Colorado."

"Anything on Donald Glass himself?"

"Nothing—and volumes. If you believe all the gossip rags, some more reliable than others, Glass has had many affairs through the years. Some of the women kept silent, some of them did not. He has been married to Marie for

twenty-five years, and if I were that woman—
I'd divorce his ass." Marty was silent for a minute. Then he added quickly, "Sorry, that wasn't
terribly professional."

"You're fine. So…he's still playing the dog,
eh?"

"One suspected affair he enjoyed was re-
portedly with Francine Renault. That hit a few
of the outlets that speculate on celebrities without using their names—avoiding legal conse-
quences. Over the years, he did pay off several
women. One accused him of sexual assault—
except, when it came to it, she withdrew all
charges. There was a settlement. But most of
these are confidential legal matters, and without due process and warrants, I can only go
so far."

"Thanks. He's been spending most of his
time and effort down at his property in Florida, right?"

"Oh, he travels. London, New York, Colorado and LA. But yes, most of the time he is
in Florida. His trips to other properties tend to
be weekends, just twice a year or so."

"Does Marie go with him?"

"It seems he does those trips alone. But, of
course, paper trails can only lead you so far,"

Marty reminded him. "I'll keep searching. I'll naturally get back to you if I find anything else that might be pertinent to your investigation."

He'd parked the car. Detectives Flannery and Lawrence had waited for him.

He reported what he'd just learned to them.

Flannery shook his head. "A man with all that Glass has... Could it be possible?"

"We have nothing as yet, so let's not go getting ourselves thrown out of the resort before we have something tangible, okay?" Brock said.

"Of course not," Flannery said, and he looked at Rachel, frowning. "You should try to get some talk time in with Donald Glass," he said.

"Are you pimping me out?" she asked him.

"Never," Flannery said. "But maybe he'll respond more easily to you on many levels."

"You mean that you doubt that he takes me seriously," Rachel said.

"Rachel, Rachel, you have a chip on your shoulder," he told her.

Brock groaned slightly.

Rachel looked at Brock and he shrugged. "You never know."

"Yes, Rachel, I'm pimping you out—whatever works," Flannery told her. "He might still think of you as the teenager who spent summers at the resort, instead of the whip-smart detective you are now. You might catch him off guard."

She grinned. "Okay, just so I know what I'm doing."

"Let's get lunch," Flannery said. "Oh, and feel free to flirt with your old beau, if need be. I'm sure you've got enough wiles to go around."

Rachel paused before they reached the house, looking at Brock. "Maybe Brock could get Maura on that one," she said.

"Maura is a civilian," he said, hoping he hadn't snapped out the words.

"Yes, but…" Rachel hesitated, glancing at Flannery, who nodded. "Everyone around here always had kind of a thing for Maura. I know that I'd be with Nils—and see him look after her longingly, even though she was a summer hire. And I'd see Glass looking at her, too, and I even think that Francine Renault was hard on her because the others seemed so crazy about her. If she could just draw Nils into conversation—with us around, of course, and see where that leads."

"We do remember that we are professionals, that we play by the book," Flannery said. "But come on, Brock, what led you to law enforcement was the knowledge that you had instincts along with drive. What made me follow your career as you moved on was…well, hell, like I said. You obviously have the instincts for it. Sometimes lines get a little blurred. I am not suggesting that we really use Maura—I'm just suggesting that she could help us chat some of these people up—with one of us right there."

Brock stared at the two of them. He didn't agree, and he didn't disagree. He was surprised by Rachel's words, but he'd been mostly oblivious to others back then. He shouldn't have been surprised by Michael Flannery's passion; he'd always known that Flannery was like a dog with a bone on this case.

Brock would never use Maura. Never.

But on the other hand she was in there interacting with all the persons of interest right now.

Twelve years ago, Maura had been with him; he had been with her. No room for doubt, and certainly, they had never thought to mistrust each other.

Now she had grown into an admirable professional—and a courteous and caring human being. And she was with him once again, although he reminded himself that they had been together just a night. There had been no promises. In the end, whether there was or wasn't a future for them didn't matter in the least. She was a civilian, and that was that.

He raised a finger in an unintentional scold. "She's never alone—never, ever, alone with any of them. With Fred Bentley, either of the Hartford brothers or Donald Glass."

"Right," Flannery said.

At his side, Rachel nodded grimly. He turned and they followed him.

"I'm starving," Rachel murmured as they entered the lobby and tempting aromas subtly made their way out and around them from the restaurant.

"Yeah, it's lunchtime," Flannery said.

"I'll join you soon," Brock told them. He headed to the desk; there was a clerk there he hadn't seen before.

"Good afternoon, sir. How can I help you?" he asked.

"You're new," Brock said.

"I am, sir."

"What happened to the young lady who was working?"

"I don't know, sir, and I don't know which young lady you might mean. Mr. Bentley gives us our schedules, sir. I'm doing split shifts, morning and night now, if I can be of assistance."

"Yes, I understand Angie Parsons is doing some filming here at the resort today. Can you direct me to where they're working now?"

"They're in the library, but they don't wish to be disturbed, sir. Sir!"

Brock turned and headed for the library.

"Sir! I shouldn't have told you. They don't want to be disturbed. Please, I have just been hired on—sir!"

Brock paused to turn back. "It's all right. I'm FBI," he said.

His being FBI didn't really mean a damned thing in this scenario. But he felt he had to say something reassuring to the clerk.

He went through the lobby and down the hallway that led to the library, in back of the café.

The door was closed.

There was a sign on it that clearly said Do Not Disturb.

Well, he was disturbed himself, so he was going to do some disturbing. He knocked on the door.

To his surprise, it opened immediately.

Marie Glass stood before him, bringing a finger to her lips. He nodded. She closed the door behind him.

Angie was holding the camera. He had arrived just before they were to begin a segment. While she loved being the director and videographer, Maura was also a natural before the camera. She smiled right into the lens and said that she was in her favorite area of the resort—the library. She was with Donald Glass, who kept the library stocked, not just here, but at all of his properties, and that he bought and developed places specifically because of unique or colorful histories.

"A true taste of life, the good, the bad and the evil," Maura said, smiling.

"Exactly, for such is life, indeed, and history can be nothing less," Glass said.

Maura knew what she was doing; Glass had been interviewed so many times in his rich life that he was apparently well aware of a good ending.

"Cut! Perfect!" Angie said. "Marie, what do you think?"

Marie smiled—her usual smile. One that maintained her dignity—and gave away nothing of her real thoughts. "Excellent. If we can just do an opening at the entry...perhaps have Fred giving the guests a welcome along with Angie." She turned and looked at Brock. "Oh, would you like to appear in a video, Brock? This was once a home away from home for you."

"No, thank you—though I would enjoy watching," he said. He looked at Maura, who was looking at him then, too. He couldn't read what she was thinking, but she had that look in her eyes that indicated there were things she had to say—but to him alone.

He glanced at Marie. "Not sure my bosses now would like it," he explained.

"Well, we can finish up then," Marie said. "Donald, dear, would you like to find Fred? He has been our general manager now for over fifteen years. He should be shown greeting Angie."

"Good thinking, my dear," Glass told his wife. "Meet you out front."

Donald left. Brock smiled, excused himself and hurried after Glass.

"Sir!"

Glass stopped and turned around with surprise. "Oh, Brock, yes, what can I do for you?" He frowned. "Have you learned anything? I caught a 'breaking news flash' about thirty minutes ago. More remains have been discovered, but those over south of Gainesville. It wasn't… Did they find one of the missing girls?"

He seemed truly concerned.

"No, sir. Whoever they found has been missing much longer. They don't have an ID yet."

"You never know if that's true, or if it's what the media was told to say."

"It's true. They have no identity on the remains yet. Indulge my concern for a moment—there was a young woman working at the front desk here. She might have been just on nights, and I may be a bit overly cautious, but I noticed you have a new hire on the desk."

"We do?"

He appeared genuinely surprised. "You'd have to ask Fred about that. I must admit, I don't concern myself much with the clerks. I worry more about the restaurants and our entertainment staff. But Fred will be able to tell you."

"Thank you."

"Have you seen Fred?"

"No, I haven't, but—"

"He's probably at lunch. I'll take a look in the restaurant. Excuse me."

Brock watched him as he went on by. The man was polite to him—always had been. But he couldn't imagine that dozens of reports were all false—the man evidently had an eye for women and an appetite for affairs.

Did he leave for tours of his other properties because he just needed to work alone, or because he needed space for casual affairs?

Or maybe he didn't really leave every time he said that he was doing so, or go exactly when and where he said that he was going.

Power and money.

Maybe Glass lured young women with those assets.

Brock hurried out front.

Maura wasn't alone. She was with Marie Glass and Angie, and they were standing in broad daylight.

He was still anxious to be with her.

More anxious to hear what it was she might have to say to him alone.

IT WASN'T THAT her work was hard, but Maura was weary—ready to be done.

Most of the videos had gone very smoothly.

Angie spoke spontaneously, and they had needed no more than three takes on any one scene that day. Maura had known what she'd wanted to say—she truly loved any library, especially one as focused and unique as the library at the Frampton Ranch and Resort.

And still, she was tired.

The idea made her smile. She was happy to be tired—because she was happy that she hadn't spent much of the previous night sleeping.

She didn't want to be overly tired that night, though!

Brock appeared on the steps of the porch before Donald Glass got there. He had an easy smile as he joined them and waited for Donald to appear with Fred Bentley.

"The Devil's Millhopper! Sounds like a place I have to see!" Angie said, smiling and looking at Brock.

He shrugged. "It's geographically fascinating—and has great displays on how our earth is always changing, how the elements and organic matter often combine to make things like sinkholes and other phenomena work. Sure— I love it out there." He laughed. "I love our mermaids, too. Weeki Wachee Springs and Weeki Wachee State Park. Absolutely beautiful—crystal clear water."

"Mermaids, eh?"

"Mermaids," he agreed politely and turned away; Glass was coming down the steps with Bentley. The stocky manager was beaming.

"I get to be in a video!" he announced.

"You do," Angie said.

"With the famous Angie Parsons," Fred said. He paused, frowning. "Or with our beautiful Maura—which is fine, too. Love our beautiful Maura."

Maura smiled. "No, sir—thank you for the compliment. You get to be with our famous and beautiful Angie."

"What do I say?" Fred asked.

Maura already knew exactly where she wanted them to stand for the afternoon light— and how she wanted them walking up the steps to the porch and the entry for the finale of the little segment.

"If you could give a welcome to the Frampton Ranch and Resort—and tell us how you've been here for fifteen years," Maura said. "Naturally, in your own words, and you can add in any bit of history you like."

She probably should have expected that something would go badly.

First, Fred froze and mumbled.

Maura smiled and coaxed him.

Then he went blank.

Then he forgot to follow Angie up the stairs at the end.

He apologized and said that he should be fired—from the video, not the property. He tried to laugh.

Maura encouraged him one more time, and they were able to get a decent video.

Brock stood nearby through the whole painful process, as did Donald and Marie. The owners—the married pair—did not stand next to each other.

Nor did they speak with each other.

And when they were done, Marie thanked Angie and Maura, bade the others good-afternoon and said that she was heading out for some shopping.

Donald thanked everyone and said that he'd be in his office.

Fred thanked Angie—then Maura.

"I was horrible. You fixed me. I guess that's what a good director does. Anyway, back to work for me. See you."

He lifted a hand and started up the steps.

"Fred," Brock said, calling him back.

"Yeah?"

"I noticed you have a new hire on the front desk."

"I do," Fred Bentley told him. "Remember when I was night clerk—well, I don't like being night clerk. Heidi didn't show up at all— and didn't call with an excuse. That's grounds for dismissal, and everyone knows it, so I left a message telling her not to come back."

"You never spoke with her?" Brock asked.

Bentley frowned. "No, I got her voice mail. She must have heard it. She never came back in."

"What's Heidi's last name and where does she live?"

"Heidi Juniper. She lives between here and Gainesville," Bentley told him. His frown deepened. "You don't think that—"

"I'll need her address and contact information," Brock said. "We'll just make sure that Heidi is irresponsible—and not among the missing."

"Of course, of course, I'll get it for you right away," Bentley told him.

When Fred was gone, Angie turned to Brock, repeating Bentley's concern. "You don't really think—"

"I don't know. I think we'll just check on her, that's all," Brock said. He looked at the two of them. "Lunch?"

"Are they still serving lunch?" Maura asked. "They do close for an hour, I think, between lunch and dinner."

"I bet they'll serve us," Angie said. She smiled broadly. "Oh, I do love it when people feel that they owe you."

She started up the steps. Maura was glad; she wanted a few minutes with Brock alone.

She believed that she'd have all night, but she needed a moment now.

But Angie stopped, looked back and sighed impatiently. "Come on! Let's not push our luck too hard, okay? I want them to keep owing me."

She was waiting.

No chance to talk.

Maura started up the stairs to the porch, grateful, at least, that Brock was with her.

Grateful, in fact, that he was simply in the world—and in her part of the world once again.

Chapter Seven

Brock saw that Michael Flannery and Rachel Lawrence were still in the restaurant when he arrived—they had taken a four top, expecting him to join them.

They hadn't expected Maura and Angie, but Michael quickly grabbed another chair and beckoned them all on over.

Angie was happy to greet them both, offering to film some of the campfire fun again with them in it. She hadn't quite figured out that law enforcement officers didn't often want their faces on video that went around to the masses—especially when they worked in plain clothes.

Both politely turned her down.

"I feel like a terrible person," Angie said. "I mean, I'd seen the news. I knew that women had been kidnapped and one had been found dead...or her remains had been found. I just didn't associate it with worrying about the central and northern areas of Florida. And the state has a huge population... Not that having a huge population makes terrible things any better, but statistically, they are bound to happen. I had no idea that the FBI and the FDLE would be staked out at the resort. But I can't tell you how glad I am. Though we did finish here today. And we went to St. Augustine yesterday. I want to see this Devil's Millhopper—the big sinkhole. But I'm not sure if Nils can go right away, and he did say that he wanted to."

Nils must have been close; as if summoned, he was suddenly behind Angie's chair. "While you're waiting to go to the Devil's Millhopper, there's some other cool stuff for Maura's cameras not far from here. Cassadaga—it's a spiritualist community, and the hotel there and a few other areas are said to be haunted. There's a tavern in Rockledge that's haunted, a theater in Tampa... It goes on and on. We can find you all manner of places."

"You need permits for some of them, advance arrangements and all," Maura reminded him.

Nils grinned. "Well, there's more here, too.

Hey, I know what we have—and near here! Caves. Yes, believe it or not, bunches of caves in Florida. Up in Marianna, but closer to us—not really far at all—Dames Cave. It's in Withlacoochee State Park, but...outside the state park, on the city edge, there's an area that's not part of any park system. Not sure who owns the land but you can trek through that area and find all kinds of caves."

Maura glanced at Brock; he knew from that look that she definitely didn't want to go off exploring caves alone with Angie.

"Caves! Cool—haunted caves? Weird caves?" Angie asked.

"Oh, yes, there's an area called Satan's Playground. Not in a state park, and not official in any way. I know that Maura and Brock know it—they used to love to go off exploring when they were working here and they had a day off," Nils said. He smiled at Angie. "I'd truly love to explore the Devil's Millhopper with you, if you don't mind waiting."

Angie leaned toward him, smiling. "I don't mind at all. We'd intended to spend several days here."

Nils nodded, apparently smitten; they might have been a match made in heaven.

"Well, hey, Nils, can we still get lunch?" Maura asked.

"No," he said. "But yes, for you. Order quickly, if you don't mind. Chef saw you come in and he said that you're going to help make him more famous, so he'll wait. But he did have a few hours off before dinner, so…"

"I ate," Angie said, smiling. "Two of Chef's lunches would be great, but I just don't think I could manage to eat a second. I suggest the mahi-mahi."

Brock looked at Nils and then Maura. "Two hamburgers?" he asked.

Rachel cast Nils a weary gaze. "Mike and I had the hamburger plate. Chef makes a great hamburger."

"Yes, hamburgers sound good," Maura said.

"Done deal," Nils told them.

When he had walked away, Flannery leaned toward Angie. "I know how important your books and your videos are to you, but for the time being, please don't go off to lonely places on your own."

"I would never go on my own," Angie said.

"Good," Rachel murmured.

"I wouldn't be alone. Maura would be with me," Angie said. She turned to watch Nils.

The chef had come out of the kitchen and they were speaking.

"Good-looking man," she murmured.

"So he is. Many women think so," Rachel said, studying something on her hand. "Anyway, the point is…"

"Don't go off anywhere alone as just two young women," Flannery said.

Angie smiled at him. "Detective Flannery, did you want to come along with us? Brock? It could be fun."

"Actually, if you want to see the caves, sure," Brock said.

Maura stared at him, surprised. She quickly looked away.

She knew that if he wanted to head out to the caves, there had to be a reason. And yes, he did have a reason.

Remains had been found not far from the caves.

And there were areas where more remains might be found, or where, with any piece of luck, the living just might be found, as well.

"Nice!" Angie said. "Great—it will be a date. Well, a weird threesome date," she added, giggling. "Unless, of course, Detective Flannery, Detective Lawrence, you two could make it?"

"We're working," Rachel reminded her sharply.

"Yes, of course," Angie said.

"And," Rachel added, "we don't want to be picking up your remains, you know."

Angie stared back at her, smiling sweetly. "Not to worry on my account. Brock will be with us, and when we go to the Devil's Millhopper, we'll be with Nils. Anyway! If you all will excuse me, I just popped in for a few minutes of the great company. We did such a good job with the video this morning that I'm dying to get into the pool."

She stood, motioning that Brock and Flannery didn't need to stand to see her go. "If you take work breaks other than food, join me when you're done."

Angie left them. When she was gone, Rachel stared at Maura.

"You *like* working with her?" Rachel asked.

"She's usually just optimistic about everything," Maura said. "And I guess she has that same feeling that most of us do, most of the time—it can't happen to me."

"Until it does," Brock murmured.

Maura glanced at Brock uncertainly. She had things to say that she hadn't been about to say in front of Angie.

"What is it?" Brock asked her. "We're working a joint investigation here—Rachel and Mike and I are on the same team."

"You want to go to the caves—really?" she asked.

She hoped he would just tell her the truth. "I want to go out to the area south of the Devil's Millhopper we talked about before. The remains today were found between the Millhopper and the caves. I think it might be a good thing to explore around there some more, though it could so easily be a futile effort," Brock told her. "People tend to think of Florida with the lights and fantasy of the beaches—people everywhere. There are really vast wildernesses up here. Remains could be…anywhere."

"It's so frustrating. Nothing makes sense, and maybe we're just creating a theory that we want to be true because we don't want more dead women, and we're all a little broken by Francine's murder. Maybe these cases are all different," Rachel said, looking over at Flannery. "One set of remains in a laundry, another in a forest where a Scout had to trip over them trying to pee. The one suggests a killer who wants to hide his victims. The other suggests a killer who likes attention and wanted to create a display. I mean, it's the saddest thing in the world, the way these last remains were discovered, by a kid…out on his night toilet rounds. Oh, sorry—you guys didn't get your food yet."

Brock waved a hand in the air and Maura smiled, looking down. She hadn't been offended.

But their hamburgers had arrived. And it wasn't how the remains had been discovered that was so disturbing—it was simply that now a second set had been found.

Rachel was looking at Brock with curiosity. "Do you think that the killer could be hiding kidnap victims in a cave or a cavern? Wouldn't that be too dangerous?"

"The better-known tourist caverns?" Brock asked. "Yes. The lesser-known caverns that are just kind of randomly outside the scope of the parks? Maybe. I don't know. He'd keeping them somewhere for days, maybe even weeks. Then there are also hundreds of thousands of warehouses, abandoned factories, paper mills…" He broke off. "I just know that there are three missing women somewhere, and I'd sure as hell like to find them while they're still just missing."

"And not dead," Flannery said grimly. He turned slightly, looking at Maura. "Do you remember anything, anything at all, from back then that might suggest anyone as being… guilty? Of killing Francine Renault."

Maura shook her head, then hesitated, glancing at Brock. He nodded slightly, and she said, "I was stunned—completely shocked—when we came upon Francine's body. When the news came out that Peter Moore had killed himself, I was already far away, and we were young and… I didn't know what else to believe. I—I was exploring on the internet today, though, and came across something that might—or might not—have bearing on this. It's a bit strange, so stick with me. There was a society in this area, decades ago, called the Sons of Supreme Being. They were suspected of the disappearance and possible death of a woman in the 1950s. That's why it struck me as maybe relevant. One of their members was supposed to testify in court—he died before he could. Now, I got this information from a random site—I haven't verified it in any way, but…"

Brock looked over at Flannery. "Have you ever heard anything about this group—this Sons of Supreme Being society or club or whatever?"

Flannery shook his head and then frowned. "Maybe, yes, years ago. I'm not sure I remember the name… When I joined the force, some of the old-timers were wondering during a murder investigation if the group might have raised its head again—a girl had been found in a creek off the Saint Johns River. She was in sad shape, as if she'd been used and tossed about like trash. But her murderer was caught—and eventually executed. Talk of rich kids picking up the throwaways died down. But as far as I know, nothing like that has been going on."

Maura was still looking at Brock.

"You have something else," he said.

She nodded and lowered her voice. "I don't think that Marie Glass realized that she was standing by me or that she was speaking aloud, but…she was watching her husband with Angie. And she said something to the effect that she shouldn't…cover for him. And she acted as if she hadn't said anything at all when she caught me looking at her. But in all fairness… Glass has always been decent to the people who worked for him, even if…"

"He's paid off a number of women through the years," Rachel said. "He was always decent to me. But there were rumors about him and Francine."

Glancing over at Maura, Brock said, "I want to find out if a young lady named Heidi Juniper is all right."

"Heidi Juniper?" Flannery asked him.

"She was working here. She didn't show up and Bentley left her a message that she was fired. He's supposed to be getting me contact information for her. Under the circumstances, I think it's important to know why Heidi didn't show up for work."

They had all finished eating. Flannery stood first. "Rachel and I will get to work finding out about Heidi Juniper. I was thinking you might want to talk to your old friends Donald and Marie Glass."

"Hardly my old friends," Brock said.

"I'm going to go to the library," Maura said. She paused, looking at them all. "It really wouldn't make sense. Donald Glass may be a philandering jerk, since he is a married man. But he is so complete with his libraries, with his campfire stories…he included Francine's murder in the collection. Would he be so open if he was hiding something?"

"Being so open may be the best way of hiding things," Flannery said. He hesitated, glancing from Brock to Maura.

"Young lady, you are a civilian. You be careful."

"Not many people think that reading in a library is living on the edge," she said, smiling. "Brock will be near, and reading is what a civilian might do to help."

"We thank you," Flannery said. "Rachel…"

She rose and the two of them headed out.

"I'm going to the library with you," Brock told Maura.

"But I thought you wanted to speak with Marie and Donald," she said.

"What do you want to bet that they both show up while we're there—separately, but…"

"You're on," she said softly, standing.

MAURA KNEW WHAT she was looking for—anything that mentioned the Sons of Supreme Being. She delved into the scrapbooks that held newspaper clippings through the decades, aiming for the 1950s. Brock was across the room, seated in one of the big easy chairs, reading a book on the different Native American tribes who had inhabited the area. It was oddly comfortable to be there with him, even though she did find her mind wandering now and then, wishing that they could forget it all—and go far from here, someplace with warm ocean breezes and hours upon hours to lie together, doing nothing but breathing in salt air and each other.

Gritting her teeth, she concentrated on her research.

After going through two of the scrapbooks that went through the 1950s, she came upon what she was seeking.

The first article was on the disappearance.

In 1953, Chrissie Barnhart, a college freshman, had disappeared. She had last been seen leaving the school library. Friends had expected her to meet up with them at the college coffee shop to attend a musical event.

She had not returned to her room.

There was a picture of Chrissie; she had been light haired and bright eyed with soft bangs and feathery tresses that surrounded her face.

The next article picked up ten days later.

In a college dorm, a young man had awakened to hear his roommate tossing and turning and mumbling aloud, apparently in the grips of a nightmare. Before he had wakened his friend, he had heard him saying, "I didn't know we were going to kill her. I didn't know we were going to kill her."

The event was reported to the police and an officer brought the student who had the nightmare in for questioning; his name had been Alfred Mansfield. At first, Mansfield had denied doing anything wrong. He'd had a nightmare, nothing more. But the police had put the fear of God into him, and in exchange for immunity, he had told them about a society called the Sons of Supreme Being. Their fathers had been supportive of Hitler's rise to power in Germany. After the war, they had made their existence a very dark secret. Only the truly elite were asked to join—elite, apparently, being the very rich.

Alfred Mansfield hadn't known who he had been with, but he was certain he could help bring those who had killed Chrissie to justice. He had simply accepted a flattering invitation, donned the garments sent to him late one night and joined with a small group, also clad in Klan-like masks, in the clearing.

All were anonymous—but he thought that their leader might have been Martin Smith, the son of a wealthy industrialist.

They hadn't killed Chrissie on the day she had been taken; Alfred didn't know where she had been kept. He only knew that he was in the clearing with the double tree when she had been dragged out, naked and screaming, and that the leader had spoken to the group about their need to make America great with the honor of those who rose above the others; to that end, they sacrificed.

Alfred had tried not to weep as he watched what was done to her and how she died. He didn't want to be supreme in any way. He wanted to forget what had happened.

He wanted the nightmares to stop.

He would serve as an informant for the police.

He was released, both he and the police believing that they had taken him in for questioning quietly and that he was safe out in the world. He'd done the right thing by letting the police know, and they would take it from there.

Alfred's body had been dragged out of the

Saint Johns River twenty-four hours after his release. He had been repeatedly stabbed before being thrown into the water to drown.

The body of Chrissie Barnhart had never been found.

Maura turned a page to see an artist's rendering of Alfred's description of the murder of the young woman.

She gasped aloud.

It was a sketch created by a police artist. But it might have been the clearing by the History Tree, looking almost exactly as it did today.

Minus the masked men.

And the naked, screaming woman, appropriately hidden behind the sweeping cloaks of the men.

"Brock… Brock…"

Maura said his name, beckoning to him, only to hear him clear his throat.

She spun around. As they had both expected to happen, a Glass had come into the room.

Marie. Brock had risen and was blocking the path between Maura and Marie.

"Mrs. Glass," Maura said, rising. She felt guilty for some reason—and she must have looked guilty. Of something. She quickly smiled and made her voice anxious as she asked, "Did we miss something? I know that Angie will be more than happy to start up again with anything else you'd like."

"Oh, no, dear, I think we did a great job today. I just heard that someone was in the library—I should have known that it was you two! My bookworms. Still, in my memory, the best young people we ever hired for our summer program," Marie said.

"Thank you," Maura said.

Marie was looking at Brock. "Such a shame," she said. "And I'm so sorry. What happened... Well, the mistake cost all of us, I'm afraid."

She did appear as if the memory caused her a great deal of pain.

"Marie, it's long over, in the past—and as far as things went, my life hardly had a ripple," Brock told her. Maura looked at him; he was so much taller than Marie that she could clearly see his face. His look might as well have been words.

She'd been much more than a ripple; losing her had been everything.

She lowered her head quickly, not wanting Marie to see her smile.

"It wasn't your fault," Maura assured her.

Marie was silent for a minute, and then said, "Maybe, maybe I could have… Um, I'm sorry. I didn't mean to disturb you. Get back to it—I have to…have to…do something. Excuse me."

She fled from the library.

"See?" Maura whispered to Brock. "See? There's something bothering her. She has, I think, been telling law enforcement that Donald was with her—*when he wasn't*. Brock, you have to come read this. Donald Glass didn't go to school here, but…if there was ever a candidate for the Sons of Supreme Being, he is one! Do you think that he could be resurrecting some old ideal? And look—look at the police sketch. Well, you have to read!"

Brock sat down where she had been. She set a hand on his shoulder, waiting while he went quickly through the clippings.

He was silent as he studied the pictures.

He turned back to her, rising, and as he did so, his phone began to ring. He pulled it from his pocket, glanced at the ID and answered. "Flannery. What did you find?"

His face seemed to grow dark as he listened. Then he hung up and looked at her.

"What is it?" she asked.

"I think we have another missing woman.

Which frightens me. I just don't know how many this killer of ours keeps alive at one time."

"I'LL BE FINE. I'll stay right next to Angie—and the group. We saw Mark Hartford in the hallway—he said that he had twenty people signed up for tonight. Oh, yeah—and Detectives Flannery and Lawrence are staying behind," Maura told Brock.

"I wish you'd just lock yourself in this room until I got back," he said, smoothing his fingers through her hair.

They hadn't slept; they weren't waking up. But they were in bed, and he was still in love with her face on the pillow next to his.

They'd left the library, making plans. But while talking, they'd headed across the lobby, to the elevator, up to her room.

And then talking had stopped, and they were kissing madly, tearing at each other's clothing, falling onto the bed, kissing each other's bodies frantically—very much like a pair of teenagers again, exploring their searing infatuation.

"Reminds me of staff bunk, Wing Room 11," she had told him breathlessly, her eyes on his as they came together at last, as he thrust into her, feeling again as he had then, as if he had found the greatest high in the world, as if nothing would ever again be as it was being with her, in her, feeling her touch and looking into her eyes.

And it never had been.

"I wonder if Mr. and Mrs. Glass ever knew how much the staff appreciated the staff room?" he'd asked later when, damp, cooling and breathing normally again, they had lain together, just touching.

Their current conversation had started with, "We have to get up. You have to go and see Heidi's family, and I'm taking my camera out for the campfire and ghost walk again."

"No. You're locking yourself in this room."

"No, that would be ridiculous. I'll be with about two dozen witnesses. No one would try anything."

The argument had been done; she did have logic in her favor. And so they dressed, reluctant to part, knowing that they must.

The evening had been decided.

Brock hesitated. "Do you think that Angie knows we're together again?"

"Probably, but…"

"But?"

"I'm not so sure she'd care. Angie is—Angie. Unabashed. Men are dogs—adorable dogs, and she loves them. But one of her great sayings is that if men are dogs, women definitely get to be bitches."

He frowned, thinking about Angie's behavior at lunch. "Does she know anything about Rachel and Nils having once been hot and heavy?"

"I don't think so. Why would she? She wasn't around way back then. Angie does like Nils. She likes you better, but…"

"I'm spoken for?"

"She might actually think that you're more interested in me—and that wouldn't sit well with her ego. She did tell me that if I wasn't interested, she'd move in."

He laughed. "Well, honesty is a beautiful thing."

"It can be—it can be awkward, too," Maura assured him. "So, are you leaving?"

"Not until I see you gathered with a large group of guests and Angie to head out to the campfire."

"Okay, then, we should go down."

He opened the door for her. They headed for

the lobby. It was busy—people were gathering. One was a family, including a mom and a dad and three children: older boys and a girl of about five. The couple from the pool was going to be at the campfire that night; they greeted Maura warmly. A few people seemed to be alone. There were two more families, one with a little girl, one with twin boys who appeared to be about fourteen.

Angie was there already, chatting with Mark.

"Hey—are you coming out tonight?" Mark asked Brock. He seemed pleased with the prospect.

"No, duty calls," Brock said. "But hopefully I'll catch up by the end."

"You have to go?" Angie asked.

"I do."

"You can't send that other cop?"

"No—because Mike Flannery and Rachel Lawrence are coming here tonight. Rachel knows all about the campfire and the walk and the stories, but Mike has never had a chance to go. And there are things I like to do myself," Brock said.

"Ah, yeah, every guy thinks he's got to do everything himself," Angie said.

"Just on this. Mike and Rachel have really been taking on the brunt of the load. My turn for an initial investigation," he said pleasantly.

He saw that Mike and Rachel had arrived.

"I'll just have a word with Mike—maybe I'll see you later."

He walked over to join Flannery and Rachel, aware that they'd be heading to the campfire any minute.

"Thanks for doing the interview tonight," Flannery said. "Really. I know you don't want to leave. I swear, we'll watch her like a pair of parental lions."

"I think male lions just lie around," Rachel said.

"I'll be a good male lion," Flannery said. "I feel that I do need to do this. Everyone really knows the stories and the tree—or trees—but me."

Brock didn't want to admit that he really wanted to interview Heidi's parents himself; there were often little things that could be said but lost in retelling. It was always better to have several interviews with family, witnesses and more. And he did owe this one to Mike.

"I'll be back as soon as possible," Brock told them.

"And really, we don't know that you need to be worried."

"I don't know. Glass is looking like a more viable suspect all the time," Brock said.

"Glass won't be out here. No need to fear," Rachel said. "And I may be small, but trust me—I am one fierce lioness."

Brock smiled. "I know," he told her.

He turned. Mark Hartford was deep in conversation with Maura. She wasn't looking Brock's way—she was listening.

He turned and headed out to the parking lot and his car. He knew he couldn't be ridiculous—he'd never keep his job that way.

It was a twenty-minute drive east to Heidi's home in a quiet neighborhood just south of St. Augustine. He noted that the girl lived in a gated estate.

The houses were about twenty years old and reflected an upper-working-class and family atmosphere.

Heidi's parents were eagerly waiting for him. Her mother, Eileen, a slim woman with curly gray hair and dark, tearstained eyes—was frantic. Heidi's father, Carl, bald and equally slim, kept trying to calm her.

"The police didn't even want to start a report

until today—they said that she hadn't really been missing. I know my daughter—when she says she's coming home, she's coming home!" Eileen said and started to cry.

"When was the last time you spoke with her?" Brock asked gently.

"She was at work. She said she was leaving soon. It was right at the end of her shift—for that day. Shifts could change, and she didn't care at all. She sometimes worked double shifts, but she said that she wasn't going to work double that day. She was tired. She was coming home. But she never arrived. I waited up. I woke Carl. We drove all up and down the highway. I mean, nothing happened to her here—our community is very secure."

"Did you call her work—talk to anyone there?"

"Some man answered the phone—he just sounded irate. He said that they weren't a babysitting service and she wasn't even with the summer program. That she probably ran off with some friends!"

"You don't know the man's name?"

"He just answered the phone, 'Front desk, how can I help you?'" Eileen said.

"Rude. If I'd known how rude… You'll investigate, right? The detective who called us—Flannery—he was the first one who seemed concerned," Carl said.

Brock nodded. "We'll take this very seriously, I swear," he assured them, taking Eileen's folded hands. "This is important. Did she say anything else? Had she been having any trouble with anyone there? Had any of the other employees or guests been ugly to her—or come on to her inappropriately?"

"She loved her job," Carl said. "Loved it." He looked at his wife. "She said that Mr. Glass was nice, but she hardly saw him. Or Mrs. Glass. Fred Bentley was her supervisor, and he seemed to be fine. She said he was a stickler for time and the rules, but she was always on time, and she never broke the rules, so they got on fine. Oh, she loved the guy who was like a social director—and she was welcome to use the pool and the gym and go on the walks—as long as she wasn't disturbing or taking anything away from the guests. There wasn't anything she told you that she wouldn't have told me, right?" Carl asked his wife. "As far as I know, she simply loved her job."

"Yes, she did," Eileen agreed. "But..."

She frowned and broke off.

"Please, tell me what you're thinking," Brock said. "Even if it seems unimportant."

Eileen's frown deepened as she exhaled a long sigh before speaking. "Something odd... She was muttering beneath her breath. She said..."

"Yes?"

"Well, I think... I'm not even sure I heard her right. The last time I talked to her on the phone—before she left work and disappeared—she said something like...'Supreme Being, my ass!' Yes, that was what she was muttering. I didn't pay that much attention—I thought she was talking about a guest—someone acting all superior. I didn't think much of it—people can act that way, when they think they're superior to those who are working. And my daughter would deal with it—and mutter beneath her breath. Yes. I'm almost positive, and honestly, I'm not sure what it can mean, if anything, but... Yes. She murmured, 'Supreme Being, my ass.'"

Chapter Eight

"The beautiful Gyselle," Mark Hartford said, "is sometimes seen in the woods near the History Tree. Running from it. A ghost forced to live where she saw the end of her life. Or, as a spirit, does she remember better times? Is she running to the tree—where she would meet her lover and dream of the things that might have been in life?"

He told the tales well, Maura thought. And even after they had finished at the campfire, he spoke as they moved along the trails into the woods, and finally, to the History Tree.

Mark had asked her to speak twice and she'd obliged; she'd had the camera rolling again, too—she might as well since they were out there. Angie could decide later which night's footage she liked best.

Maura noted with a bit of humor that Mike

and Rachel were being true to whatever promises they had certainly given Brock—they hadn't been ten full feet away from her all night.

But at the tree, she found that she wanted it on video from every angle. She kept picturing the police artist's rendering she had seen that day.

Creepy figures surrounding the tree, unidentifiable. The victim from the 1950s, Chrissie, caught in the arms of one of her attackers.

Were the current victims being held—as she had been held? And if so, how in the hell were they being hidden so well…until their remains were left to rot in the elements?

"You are getting carried away," Angie whispered to her.

"Just a little," Maura agreed.

"Questions—anything else?" Mark asked his group pleasantly.

Maura wondered if she should or shouldn't speak, but her mouth opened before her mind really worked through the thought.

"Yes, hey, Mark, have you ever heard of a group called the Sons of Supreme Being?" she asked.

He looked at her, a brow arching slowly.

His entire tour group had gone silent, all curious at her question.

"Yeah," he said. "I—yeah. I thought it was kind of a rumored thing." He lifted a hand. "No facts here, folks, just stuff I heard at college. They say they existed once. They were a pack of snobs—thought they were better than anyone else. They were never sanctioned by any of the state schools—in fact, I heard you got your butt kicked out if you were suspected of being one of them. They were like an early Nazi-supporter group—seemed they watched what Hitler was doing in the 1930s. But, hey, nothing like that exists now, trust me!" He grinned at his crowd. "I'm a people person. Someone would have told me. Where did you hear about them?"

"Oh, I read something," Maura said. "I was just curious if it had been real or not."

"I can't guarantee it, but I heard that they did exist. No one I know has anything on who the members might have been or anything like that," Mark told her. "Although I did hear that while the rumors of the group started in the 1930s, it really went further back—like way, way back. It was the rich elite even in the 1850s—dudes who came to Florida from the north and all, and built plantations and homes and ranches after Florida became a territory and then a state. They considered themselves to be above everyone else—everyone! If you ask me—a theory I've never spoken aloud before—I have a feeling that Gyselle's death might have been helped along by members—even way back then. Those dudes would have thought that this tree was a sacred spot. And Julie Frampton could have easily whispered into someone's ear. Gotten them to do the deed."

"There is an idea for you," Maura murmured. "Thanks, Mark."

She felt Detective Flannery take a step closer to her.

"Okay, time to head on back, folks. No stragglers—no stragglers. We don't know what's up, but we're asking people to stay close." Mark pointed to the way out.

His group obediently headed back along the trail.

As they came out of the woods, she saw that Brock was walking from the parking lot toward them. "Brock!" Angie called. "You missed new stuff—the beautiful Gyselle might have been killed by a secret society. Wild, huh?"

Brock frowned and glanced past her at Maura, Mike and Rachel.

"I asked Mark if he'd ever heard of the group," Maura said.

"Oh," he said. "Well, you got something new and fresh on a tour. Great."

He wasn't going to talk, not there, not then— not with others around them. She thought, too, that he seemed tense.

Maybe even with her.

Because, perhaps, she shouldn't have spoken.

But the day was done at last; she wanted nothing more than to get back and close out the world—except for Brock.

She knew that he'd meet first with Mike and Rachel. And, she knew, he'd probably had a rough last few hours—talking to the parents of another girl who had disappeared.

She yawned. "Long, long day—I'm going up to bed," she said. "Angie, we can head out to those caverns tomorrow—at least, I think we can. Brock, can you take the time?"

"Yes. In fact, I think that maybe Detectives Flannery and Lawrence can join us."

Flannery might have been taken by surprise; if so, he didn't show it.

"Yes, we'll all go. Search those woods—close to where the last remains were discovered. You okay with that, Angie?"

"You bet—that will be perfect. Oh, I do hope we find something!" she said enthusiastically. "Oh, lord, that sounded terrible. Terrible. I mean, I didn't mean it that way. Except, of course, it would be cool to find a lair, a hideout—save someone!"

"That would be something exceptional," Maura said, looking at Brock. He still seemed disturbed. "So," she added, "Angie, an excursion tomorrow means you have to wake up fairly early."

"Oh, I will, I will. Meet in the coffee shop at 8:30 a.m.?" she asked.

"Sounds good," Brock said.

"Adventure day—nice break," Rachel murmured.

"You're really going to be there at eight thirty?" Maura asked skeptically.

"Ah, and I even have plans tonight! But yes, I'll be there," Angie said.

"You have plans tonight?" Brock asked her.

"Not to worry—I'm not leaving the property. I'm just meeting up with a new friend in the coffee shop—or not the actual coffee shop, you know, the little kiosk part that stays open 24/7. We'll be fine."

Maura wanted to get away from everyone.

"Okay," Maura said. "I am for bed." She didn't wait for more; she hurried past them and straight for the resort, anxious to get to her room.

And more anxious for Brock to join her.

BROCK REMAINED OUTSIDE, just at the base of the porch steps, with Mike and Rachel—waving as Angie at last left them, smiling and hurrying on up the steps to meet her date.

He quickly filled them in on what Heidi's parents had told him.

Flannery shook his head. "It just gets more mired in some kind of muck all the time. I can see a serial kidnapper and killer, but… You think that there's some idiot Nazi society that has been going on for years—oh, wait, even before there were Nazis?"

"I know, I never heard of it before today—and then that's all that I've heard about. So there is a cult—or someone wants us all to believe that there is," Brock said.

"That could mean all kinds of people are involved," Rachel mused. She frowned. "I never

heard what Mark was saying tonight before—
that a really narcissistic group being 'supreme'
might have existed as far back as the end of
the Seminole Wars. Seriously, come on, think
about it—and let's all be honest about human-
ity. At that time, males were superior, no hint
of color was acceptable and no one had to say
they were or weren't supreme. Society and
laws dictated who was what."

"Okay, historically, we know that Gyselle
was dragged out of the house to the hanging tree and basically executed there. History
never told us just who did the dragging," Brock
said. "I do believe that Heidi was taken by the
same people who took the other girls—and I
don't believe that she's dead yet, and we can
only really pray—and get our asses moving—
to find them."

"Brock, we have had officers going into any
abandoned shack or shed, getting warrants for
anything that was suspicious in the least. The
state has been moving, but yeah, we need to
get going on the whole instinct thing. You
think that the caverns might yield something?"

"I think that remains were found very close
to them," Brock said. "Anyway, I'm going up
for the night. I'll see you in the morning."

"Yep. We'll say good-night and see you in the morning," Flannery said.

By then, the group from the campfire tales and walk had apparently retired for the night. The lobby was quiet as Brock walked across it.

The young man he'd met the night before was on the desk. Brock waved and headed for the elevator, but then noted that he didn't see Angie or the date she was meeting.

He headed to the desk.

"Yes, sir, how may I help you?" the young clerk asked.

"Miss Parsons was down here, I believe. I think she was meeting up with someone in that little twenty-four-hour nook by the entrance to the coffee shop. I don't see her."

"She was down here… I guess she went up."

"Was she alone?"

"I… I said hello, and then I was going through the reservations for tomorrow and okaying a few late departures. I didn't really notice."

Angie's room was on his way to the attic floor. Brock could knock on her door and check on her.

According to what he had seen and learned from Maura, Angie might well have cut to the chase with whomever she had met.

She might be in her room—occupied.

Well, hell, too bad. He was going to have to check on her—whether he interrupted something intimate or not.

MAURA WASN'T SURE what was taking Brock so long, except that he'd be filling Mike and Rachel in on whatever had gone on with Heidi's parents.

She paced her room for a few minutes, then paused as her phone rang.

She answered quickly, thinking it was Brock.

It was not.

It was Angie.

"Maura," Angie said. "You've got to come out—find Tall, Dark and Very Studly, and come on out here."

"Come on out here? Angie, where are you?"

Angie giggled. "Almost getting lucky!" she said in a whisper. "You need to come out here—first. I've found something. Or rather, my own Studly found something for me. Come on, quickly, just grab Brock and get out here."

"Out here where?"

"The History Tree. I have something for you!"

Maura heard a strange little yelping sound—excitement or a scream? She dropped the phone and hurried out into the hallway, just in time to see Brock coming up the stairs at the end.

"Brock, come on. We have to go." Maura said.

"I tried to check on Angie because I didn't see her in the lobby, but she's not answering her door," he told her.

"She isn't there. She's out at the History Tree. Brock—she said that she's found something. She was excited, but then, it was strange—come on!"

She didn't wait for the elevator—she headed straight for the stairs. He followed behind her, calling her name.

"You shouldn't go. I should go alone. Maura!"

He didn't catch up with her until they were out on the lawn, halfway out to the campfire and the trail. He caught her by the arm. "Let me go—you get back in the resort, up in your room—locked in."

"I don't think there's anything wrong," Maura said. "She wanted me to see something. Brock, you're armed and she said to bring you. She just wanted us both to come."

He shook his head, staring at her, determined.

"It could be a trap."

"Angie sounded like Angie. What kind of a trap would that be? Come on."

"No! You don't know—go back into the resort, into your room and lock the door."

She stared back at him.

"Please, Maura, if we're to go on…"

"But, Brock, I just talked to her. This is silly. I'm with you, and… Please, let's just hurry!"

She broke away from him, but he overtook her quickly. "Maura!"

"What?"

"You can't put yourself in danger," he told her. "Let me do my job."

"Oh, all right!"

"Go!"

She did. And since she knew that he'd wait until he saw her heading back into the resort, she turned and headed for the steps.

Something was bugging her about Angie's call. There had been that strange little noise. And then Angie hadn't spoken again. The line had gone dead.

Irritated but resolved, she hurried back into the resort. She waved to the night clerk and headed to the elevator—too tired and antsy for the stairs.

She walked down the hallway, feeling for

her phone to try calling Angie again. She remembered that she'd dropped her phone on her bed.

That was all right; she was almost there.

She walked down the hallway to her room and pushed open the door.

The room was dark.

She hadn't left the lights out.

And neither had she thought to lock the door.

She had no idea what hit her; something came over her head, smothering any cry for help she might have made, and then she hit the floor.

And darkness was complete.

BROCK WALKED CAREFULLY through the woods, swiftly following the trail to the History Tree but hugging the foliage and staying in the shadows.

Long before he reached the tree, he heard the cries for help and the sobs. He quickened his pace, but continued to move stealthily.

When he reached the clearing, he saw that Angie was tied to the tree.

She hadn't been hanged as the long-ago Gyselle had been; she was bound to the massive trunk of the conjoined trees, sobbing, crying out.

Brock didn't rush straight to her; he surveilled the clearing and the surrounding areas the best he could in the darkness. The moon was only half-full, offering little help.

There seemed to be no one near Angie. Still, he didn't trust the scene. It made no sense. Girls disappeared. Months later, remains were found.

None had been tied to the History Tree.

He pulled his phone out and called Flannery. "History Tree—backup," he said quietly.

And then, with his Glock at the ready, he made his way forward, still waiting for a surprise ambush from the bushes.

"Brock, Brock! Be careful, he knows you're coming... He knows... He could be here, here somewhere..."

"I'm watching, Angie," he said, reaching her. He found his pocketknife to start sawing on the ropes that bound her to the tree.

When she was free, she threw herself into his arms. "You saved me. Thank God I called Maura. He might have come back. He might have... He would have killed me. Oh, Brock, thank you, thank you."

Mike and Rachel came bursting into the clearing.

Angie jerked back, frightened by their arrival.

"It's all right, Angie. It's all right—who brought you here? Who the hell brought you here?" Brock demanded.

She began to shake. "I don't believe it! I still don't believe it!" she said, and she began to sob.

MAURA AWOKE TO DARKNESS. For a moment, the darkness confused her.

At first she had no recollection of what had happened. When she did start to remember—it wasn't much. Someone had attacked her when she'd walked into her room.

She touched her head. No blood, but she had one hell of a headache.

Brock had been right. The call had been a trap.

Angie had called…and there had been that little yelp, and then the phone had gone dead. But Brock hadn't allowed her to go with him.

Whoever had done this knew how Brock would react. Knew that he would never allow Maura to chance her own life.

She didn't know who it was. Mark or Nils Hartford? Bentley?

Donald Glass himself?

She tried to move and was surprised that she could. She struggled her way out of the covering that all but encased her. It was a comforter—the comforter from her bed at the resort.

She struggled to sit up and realized the earth around her was cold—as if she were in the ground. Struggling, she sat up—but she couldn't stand. The space was too tight. She could see nothing at all.

On her hands and knees, she began to crawl, blinking, trying to adjust to the absolute darkness. Where was Angie—had they taken her, too? Had Brock raced out to the clearing—to find nothing?

If so...

He'd wake the very dead to get every cop in the state out to start looking.

Maura began to shake, terrified. Then, wincing at the pain in her head, she moved forward again.

Brock would search for her, she knew.

She also needed to do her damned best to save herself.

She paused for a minute, listening. Nothing—but it was night. Late at night. She breathed in.

Earth. Earth and...

She paused, and suddenly she knew where she was—well, not where she was, but what she was in. There was earth, but she'd also touched something hard, a bit porous.

And native to a nearby area. Coquina. A sedimentary rock made of fossilized coquina shells that had been used in the building of the great fort in St. Augustine, that still graced walkways and garden paths and all manner of other projects. But to the best of her knowledge, there hadn't been any at the Frampton Ranch and Resort, unless it had been long, long ago.

Maybe she was no longer near the resort. She didn't know how long she had been unconscious.

She kept crawling, not even afraid of what night creatures might be sharing this strange underground space with her.

And then, suddenly, she touched flesh.

"Who, Angie? Who did this to you?" Brock demanded, his arm around her still-shaking body as they headed back toward the resort.

Flannery and Rachel had searched the area, a call had been put out for a forensic team and cops would soon be flooding the place.

"It was—it was Donald Glass!" she said, still sounding incredulous. "He was so polite, so gracious, and he said that he wanted me to see something very special. It was him!"

Flannery, right behind them, pushed forward. "Let's see if the old bastard is at the house. Supreme Being. I'll bet he sure as hell thinks that he's one. What the hell was he going to do? Did he think that Angie would die by herself by morning? Or was he coming back to finish the deed—right where he probably murdered Francine years ago?"

As they neared the house, Brock called to Rachel. "Stay with Angie, will you? I've got to go and bring Maura down."

"Don't leave me!" Angie begged, grabbing his arm.

He freed himself. "I have to get Maura."

Rachel had gotten strong; she managed to help Brock disengage a terrified Angie.

Brock raced up the stairs to Maura's room. He could tell the door to her room was open from halfway down the hall. He sprinted into it.

Empty.

The comforter was gone from the bed; her phone lay on the floor.

The breath seemed to be sucked out of him. His heart missed a beat, and for a split second, he froze.

It had been a trap. And he'd been such an ass, he hadn't seen it.

By the time he raced downstairs, the terrified desk clerk was hovering against the wall and Flannery had Donald Glass—in a smoking jacket—in handcuffs.

"No, no, this is wrong—I've been in my room. Ask my wife! Angie! Why the hell would you say these things, accuse me? I did nothing to you. I opened my resort to you. I… Why?"

Angie was shaking and crying, but Donald Glass was agitated, too. He appeared wild-eyed and confused.

"You meant to kill me!" Angie cried.

"I've been in my room all night!" Glass bellowed. "Ask my wife!"

Marie Glass was coming down the stairs, her appearance that of a woman who was stunned and stricken. Her hands shook on the newel post of the grand stairway as she reached the landing.

"Marie, tell them!" Glass bellowed.

Marie began to stutter. Tears stung her eyes. "I—I can't lie for you anymore, Donald."

"What?" he roared.

Brock strode up to him, face-to-face, his voice harsh, his tension more than apparent. "Where's Maura?" he demanded.

"Maura?" Glass asked, puzzled. Then he cried out, "Sleeping with you, most probably!"

"She's gone—she was taken. Where the hell is she?"

Donald Glass began to sob. He shook his white head, far less than dignified then. "I didn't take Maura. I didn't hurt Angie. I swear, I was in my room. I was in my room. I was in my room—"

"Get every cop you can. We have to search everywhere. Maura is with those other girls, I'm certain, and they're near here," Brock said.

A siren sounded, and then a cacophony of sirens filled the night.

"We'll get him to jail—you can join the hunt," Flannery told Brock.

"I'll get out to the car with him. By God, he's going to talk." Brock said. He set a hand hard on Donald Glass's shoulder, following him and Flannery out to the police cruiser.

A uniformed officer jumped out of the driver's seat and opened the back door for them.

"He's not going to talk, Brock, get on the search—" Flannery began. "Or don't," he said as Brock shoved Glass into the rear of the car and then crawled into the seat next to him.

"I don't have her. I don't have her. I don't have her!" Donald Glass screamed. "Don't kill me. Please, don't kill me!"

"I'm not going to kill you," Brock said. "What I need to know from you is anything I don't. Where around here could someone hide women?"

"But I swear, I didn't—"

"You—or anyone else. Dammit, man, I'm trying to believe you! Talk to me."

"WATER…PLEASE… Don't kill me… Water…"

The flesh Maura had encountered spoke.

"I don't have water. I'm not going to kill you," Maura assured the voice she heard. "I'm Maura Antrim. Who are you?"

"Maura!"

The person struggled in the darkness. Maura felt hands grab for her. "I know you… I know you… I'm Heidi… I'm so scared! I stopped because a car had flashing lights and… I went out to help and there was no one to help, and someone hit me, and… I'm dying, I'm sure. I'm going to die down here. I'm so scared. It's so dark. I don't know… Did they take you, too?"

"Yes, they hit me over the head in my hotel room. You don't have any idea of who did this to you?"

Maura felt the girl shake her head.

"We're not far from the resort—I know that. Not far at all."

"But where…?"

"I think we're in a bit of a sinkhole—covered up years and years ago—but someone used it as something. They shored up the sides with coquina. But they got us in here—there has to be a way out. Can you still move?"

"Barely."

"Okay, so stay still. I'm going to try to find a way to escape."

"No! Don't leave me!" Heidi begged, clinging to her.

"Then you have to come with me," Maura said firmly.

She began to crawl again, and she felt the earth grow wetter.

They were in a drainage culvert. They were

probably right off the main highway, and if she could just find the grating…

Her mind was numb, and it was also racing a hundred miles an hour. Angie had called her because she had been meeting someone. That someone had lured Angie out and let her lure Brock out and, of course…

That someone had known Brock. Yes, she'd thought that right away. Known that he would make her go back, that he'd consider himself trained, ready to meet danger.

Brock would want Maura safe.

Whoever it had been walked easily and freely through the resort, knew where to go—how to avoid the eyes of the desk clerk and the cameras that kept watch on the lobby.

Thoughts began to tumble in her mind. One stuck.

It couldn't be. And, of course, it was just one someone…

It wasn't a society or an organization—but rather someone who had known about it.

She suddenly found herself thinking about the long-lost Gyselle, the beautiful woman running from her pursuers, those who would hang her from the History Tree until dead.

Maybe they had been part of a society. Maybe they hadn't. Maybe they had just...

She saw a light! A tiny, tiny piece of light...

THE NIGHT WAS ALIVE. Police were searching everywhere.

Dogs were out, each having been given a whiff of Maura's scent. But while they searched the woods and the house and the gardens and the pool, Brock headed off toward the road.

Donald Glass had spilled everything he knew. No, there had never been a basement; there were foundations, of course, but barely wide enough for one maintenance man. There had been a well, yes, filled in years and years ago.

Outbuildings had been torn down. The wings on the resort were new. There were no hidden houses; the one little nearby cemetery had no mausoleums or vaults...

Where to hide someone?

Warehouses aplenty on the highway. And the drainage tank off the road, ready to absorb excess water when hurricanes came tearing through.

A perfect place for a body to deteriorate quickly.

Donald Glass had been taken off to jail.

That didn't matter to Brock right now. Nothing mattered.

Except that he find Maura.

He reached the road and raced alongside the highway, seeking any entrance to the sunken areas along the pavement.

He ran and ran, and then ran back again, and then noted an area where foliage had been tossed over the drain.

He raced for it.

And as he neared, he heard her. Crying out, thundering against the metal grate.

"Maura!"

He cried her name, surged to the grate and fell to his knees. His pocketknife made easy work of the metal joints. He pulled her out and into his arms, and for a long moment, she clung to him.

And then he heard another cry.

"Heidi—she says there are other women down there… Dead or alive, I don't know."

He pulled Heidi from the drain. She crushed him so hard in a hug that he fell back, and several long seconds passed in which it seemed they were all laughing and crying.

Then, in the distance, he heard the baying of a dog. He shouted, "Over here!" Soon, there were many officers there, many dogs, and he was free to take Maura into his arms and hold her and not let go.

Epilogue

"You know," Maura said, probably confusing everyone gathered in the lobby of the Frampton Ranch and Resort by being the one to speak first. "Sometimes, really, I can still see her—or imagine her—the beautiful Gyselle, running in the moonlight, desperate to live. Legends are hard to shake. And I'm telling you this, and starting the explanation because, in one way, it's my story. And because Gyselle's life has meaning, and legends have meaning, and sometimes we don't see the truth because what we see is the legend."

She saw interest on the faces before her. The employees knew by now that Donald Glass had been taken away. They knew that horrible things had happened the night before, that Angie had been attacked by her host and that Maura had been attacked—but found, and found along with Heidi and the other three missing girls. Heidi was already fine and home with her parents. The other girls were still hospitalized. For Lily Sylvester it would be a long haul. She'd been in the dark, barely fed and given dirty water for months—and it had taken a toll on her internal organs. Lydia Merkel would most probably be allowed to go home that afternoon, and for Amy Bonham the hospital stay would be about a week.

There was hope for all of them. They'd lived.

The resort guests had all gone. They had been asked to vacate by the police and Marie Glass until the tragedy had been appropriately handled.

The resort was empty except for the staff, Detectives Flannery and Lawrence, and Angie and Maura.

Donald Glass remained gone—biding his time in jail before arraignment. But if things tonight went the way Maura thought they would, that arraignment would never come.

"Thinking about Gyselle brings to mind— to many of us—what happened to Francine Renault. Well, I don't really see her in a long gown running through the forest, but she, too, met her demise on this ranch. And through the years, we suspect, so did many other young women. They didn't all come to the tree. After Francine they were stabbed. Yes, by the same killer. Brutally stabbed to death. As Peter Moore, a cook here back then, was stabbed. It doesn't sound as if it should all relate. One killer, two killers, working independently—or together? All compelled by just one driving motive—revenge."

Blank faces still greeted her. She wasn't a cop or FBI. They were curious, but confused.

"I thought they were random kidnappings," someone murmured.

"Yes and no," Maura said.

Brock stepped forward. "We discovered a longtime association or society. It was called Sons of Supreme Being. They don't—we believe—really exist anymore. So legend gave way to what might be revamped—and imitated."

"I thought the police were going to explain what really went on here," Nils Hartford said.

"I guess Donald Glass did consider himself a supreme being," his brother added sadly.

"Well, he might have," Maura said. "But... there you go. I'm back to beautiful Gyselle, running through the forest. Her sin being that of a love affair with the owner of the plantation."

"I'm letting Maura do the explaining," Brock said. "She's always been a great storyteller."

Maura turned and looked at Marie Glass. "Donald didn't kill Francine, Marie. You did."

"What?" Marie stared at her indignantly. "I did not kill Francine. My husband killed Francine."

"No, no, he didn't. He didn't kill Francine. Nor did he kill Maureen Rodriguez or the other woman whose remains have been found. Donald loved history—and kept it alive. He loved women. You found your way to take revenge on those who led him astray—and, of course, on Donald himself. Oh, and you killed Peter Moore—that's when you discovered just how much you enjoyed wielding a knife."

"This is insane! How do you think that I—" Marie gestured to herself, demonstrating that she was indeed a tiny woman "—could manage such acts? Oh, you ungrateful little whore!"

"No need to be rude," Brock said. "Marie, you were good—but we have you on camera."

"Really? How did I tie up Angie and get back and…"

"Oh, you didn't tie up Angie."

"Of course not!"

"Angie tied herself up," Brock said calmly.

Angie sprang to her feet. "No! I wasn't even around when Francine Renault was killed. Or the cook. Why on earth do you think that I could be involved?"

"I still don't know why you were involved, Angie," Brock said. "But you were. There was no one else in the woods. We've found sound alibis for everyone else here. Oh, both Mark and Nils Hartford were sleeping with guests that night—a no-no. But you weren't one of those guests. And there's video—the security camera picked it up—of Fred Bentley talking to the night clerk right when it was all going on. What? Did you two think that we were getting close? That we'd figure it out— that Marie's hints about her husband were a little too well planted? Then, of course, there was you—wanting to see where the bones had been discovered. Strange, right? But I'm thinking that the bones washed out in the drainage system somehow—and Marie panicked and wrapped them in hotel sheets, thinking she could dispose of the remains with the laundry. And maybe you were hoping that you hadn't messed up somehow. Maybe you didn't know. But for whatever reason, you and Marie have been kidnapping and killing people. Marie getting her rage out—certain she could frame her husband if it came to it. But you..."

"That's absurd!" Angie cried.

"No, no, it's not. We checked your phone records—you talked to Marie over and over again during the last year. Long conversations. She chose the victims. You helped bring them down."

The hotel staff had all frozen, watching—as if they were caught in a strange tableau.

"You're being ridiculous!" Angie raged. She looked like a chicken, jumping up, arms waving at her sides in fury. "No, it was Marie! I didn't—"

"Oh, shut up!" Marie cried. "I'm not going down alone. I can tell you why—she wanted to hurt Donald as badly as I did. We were willing to wait and watch and eventually find a way to create proof that made the system certain that it was Donald. And those women... Whores! They deserved to suffer. We could have seen that Donald rotted for years before he got the death penalty. There's no record of it—her mother was one of my husband's whores. He paid her off very nicely to have an abortion. The woman took the money— she didn't abort." She looked at Angie. "You should have been an abortion!"

"Oh, Marie, you lie, you horrible bitch!"

Angie tore toward her in a fury.

Rachel stepped up, catching her smoothly and easily, swinging an arm across her shoulders.

She then snapped cuffs on Angie.

And Marie—dignified Marie—was taken by Mike.

She spit at him. She called him every vile name Maura had ever heard.

And then some.

They were taken out. The employees stood in silence, gaping.

Then, suddenly, everyone burst into conversation, some expressing disbelief, some arguing that they were surprised.

"No," Fred Bentley said simply, staring after them. "No."

"Yes. You saw," Brock told him.

"So, what do we do now?" Mark asked.

"Well, Donald Glass is being released. Right now he's sick and horrified at what has happened. He believed that he caused Marie to be cruel. He never knew he had an illegitimate child, and now he's left with the fact that his child…became a killer. He needs time. He's the one who has to make the decisions," Brock said. "For now, he has said to let you know that you don't need to worry while he regroups— everyone will be paid for the next month, no matter what."

There was a murmur of approval, and then slowly the group began to break up.

Fred stared at Brock and Maura for a long time. "Well," he said. "I will be here. I will keep the place in order. Until I know what Donald wants. I'll see that the staff maintain it. I'll be here for—for anything anyone may need." He started to walk away, and then he came back. "I'm… I can't believe it. Imagine, that cute little Angie. Who could figure…? But thank you, Brock. Yeah, thank you so much."

He turned and left, heading behind the restaurant toward the office.

Brock and Maura stood alone in the center of the lobby.

"Shall we go?" he asked her.

"We shall, but…"

"But where, you ask?" Brock teased. "An island. Somewhere with a beautiful beach.

Somewhere we can lie on the sand and make up for lost time, hurt for those who died and be grateful for those who lived. You are packed and ready to leave?"

"I am," she told him.

They drove away.

MAURA COULD FEEL the deliciousness of the sea breeze. It swept over her flesh, filtering through the soft gauze curtains that surrounded the bungalow. She could hear the lap of the waves, so close that she could easily run out on the sand and wade into the water.

It was beautiful. Brock had found the perfect place in the Bahamas. It was a private piece of heaven, and no one came near them unless they summoned food or drink with the push of a button. The next bungalow was down the beach, and they were separated by palms and sea grapes and other oceanfront foliage.

It was divine.

Though nothing was more divine than sleeping beside Brock so easily, flesh touching, sometimes just lying together and talking about the years gone by, and sometimes, starting with just the slightest brush against each other, making love.

There would be four days of this particular heaven, but…

"You did talk to your parents, right?" Brock asked Maura.

"Of course! If news about what happened had reached them and they hadn't heard from me…they would have been a bit crazy," Maura assured him. She inched closer to him. "I almost feel bad for my mother—she's so horrified, and she admitted all the messages she'd gotten from you and kept from me…poor thing. And then, I have myself to blame, too. I was hurt that I didn't hear from you—and so I never tried to contact you myself. I thought I was part of your past—a past you wanted closed."

"Never. Never you," he said with a husky voice. Then he smiled again. "But your mom… She is coming to the wedding."

Maura laughed. "Oh, yes. She didn't even try telling me that we were rushing things when I said we were in the Bahamas but coming home to a small wedding in New York at an Irish pub called Finnegan's. And my dad… Well, he thinks that's great. Why wait after all this time? Now or never, in his mind. It's nice, by the way, for your friend to arrange a wedding and reception in one at his place—his place? Her place?"

"Kieran and Craig have been together a long time. Craig is a great coworker and friend. Kieran owns Finnegan's with her brothers—they're thrilled to provide for a small wedding and reception. And you...you don't mind living in New York? For now? Maybe one day, we'll be snowbirds, heading south for the winter. And maybe, when we're old and gray, we'll come home for good. Or, hell, maybe I'll get a transfer. But for now..."

She leaned over and kissed him. "I lost you for twelve years. I'm going to say those vows and move to New York without blinking," she promised. "Besides... Hmm. I'm going to be looking for some new clients—New York seems like a good place to find them."

He smiled, and then he rolled more tightly to her, his face close as he said, "It's amazing. I knew I loved you then. And I never stopped loving you—and I swear, I will love you all the rest of my years, as well. With or without you, I knew I loved you."

"That's beautiful," she whispered. "I love you, too. Always have, always will." She smoothed back his hair.

He caught her hand and kissed it.

Then the kissing continued.

And the ocean breeze continued to caress them both as the sun rose higher in the sky.

Later, much later, Maura knew that the ocean breeze wouldn't be there every morning. They wouldn't be sleeping in an oceanfront bungalow with the sea and sand just beyond them.

And it wouldn't matter in the least.

Because his face would be on the pillow next to hers, every morning, forever after.

* * * * *

Get 4 FREE REWARDS!

We'll send you 2 FREE Books plus 2 FREE Mystery Gifts.

Harlequin Presents® books feature a sensational and sophisticated world of international romance where sinfully tempting heroes ignite passion.

FREE Value Over **$20**

YES! Please send me 2 FREE Harlequin Presents® novels and my 2 FREE gifts (gifts are worth about $10 retail). After receiving them, if I don't wish to receive any more books, I can return the shipping statement marked "cancel." If I don't cancel, I will receive 6 brand-new novels every month and be billed just $4.55 each for the regular-print edition or $5.80 each for the larger-print edition in the U.S., or $5.49 each for the regular-print edition or $5.99 each for the larger-print edition in Canada. That's a savings of at least 11% off the cover price! It's quite a bargain! Shipping and handling is just 50¢ per book in the U.S. and $1.25 per book in Canada.* I understand that accepting the 2 free books and gifts places me under no obligation to buy anything. I can always return a shipment and cancel at any time. The free books and gifts are mine to keep no matter what I decide.

Choose one: ☐ **Harlequin Presents®**
Regular-Print
(106/306 HDN GNWY)

☐ **Harlequin Presents®**
Larger-Print
(176/376 HDN GNWY)

Name (please print)

Address   Apt. #

City   State/Province   Zip/Postal Code

Mail to the **Reader Service:**
IN U.S.A.: P.O. Box 1341, Buffalo, NY 14240-8531
IN CANADA: P.O. Box 603, Fort Erie, Ontario L2A 5X3

Want to try 2 free books from another series! Call 1-800-873-8635 or visit www.ReaderService.com.

*Terms and prices subject to change without notice. Prices do not include sales taxes, which will be charged (if applicable) based on your state or country of residence. Canadian residents will be charged applicable taxes. Offer not valid in Quebec. This offer is limited to one order per household. Books received may not be as shown. Not valid for current subscribers to Harlequin Presents books. All orders subject to approval. Credit or debit balances in a customer's account(s) may be offset by any other outstanding balance owed by or to the customer. Please allow 4 to 6 weeks for delivery. Offer available while quantities last.

Your Privacy—The Reader Service is committed to protecting your privacy. Our Privacy Policy is available online at www.ReaderService.com or upon request from the Reader Service. We make a portion of our mailing list available to reputable third parties that offer products we believe may interest you. If you prefer that we not exchange your name with third parties, or if you wish to clarify or modify your communication preferences, please visit us at www.ReaderService.com/consumerschoice or write to us at Reader Service Preference Service, P.O. Box 9062, Buffalo, NY 14240-9062. Include your complete name and address.

HP19R3

THE FORTUNES OF TEXAS COLLECTION!

Treat yourself to the rich legacy of the Fortune and Mendoza clans in this remarkable 50-book collection. This collection is packed with cowboys, tycoons and Texas-sized romances!

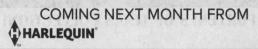